For Patia —

I look forward
to seeing your book

PLY

OH DON'T YOU CRY FOR ME

STORIES BY PHILIP SHIRLEY

ISBN: 978-0980016406
Library of Congress Control Number: 2008922596

Book Cover Design by Bill Porch
Book Interior Design by Irene Archer
Editing by Henry Oehmig

First Printing April 2008
Printed in Tennessee

Published by Jefferson Press

j e f f e r s o n
p r e s s

808 Scenic Highway
Lookout Mountain, TN 37350

In memory of Don Purvis.
I miss you, buddy.
And I pray there's a Harley in heaven
and your tank stays always full.

Contents

Charisma

Charisma squirmed in the seat from her butt stinging and leaned against the Cadillac door to get as far as possible from the preacher. The lilt of his voice left no doubt she'd often heard it before. She avoided his eyes, but watched his hands. The preacher tugged the monogrammed cuff of his left sleeve, then extended his arm over the steering wheel. He snapped his head to the side to make his neck crack, reminding her of the stepfather she'd run away from.

Sweat spots showed through the preacher's starched blue shirt from the ten minutes they'd spent outside the car under a cloudless summer sky. His hair was black and slicked back, too black to be natural, she thought. Not a strand out of place. He kept his eyes straight ahead, ignoring the expanse of mile after mile of flat fields, but placed his right hand on the worn leather Bible between them on the white leather seats. She waited silently.

Finally, he cleared his throat. "Ladies don't hitchhike," he said without looking over at her. "How old are you?"

She looked at his pristine nails tapping the Bible. A man with a manicure. She'd never seen a man who cared for the appearance of his hands. She tried to remember if she'd ever seen her boyfriend's nails when they were not black from engine grease.

"I'm eighteen," she said, since her birthday was in a month and she'd been saying she was eighteen for two years anyway.

"I should just put you out right here," he said.

She watched the speedometer and saw that he didn't slow down. His lips moved, but little sound came out. She realized he was praying. "Get thee behind me Satan," he mumbled, his eyes still ahead.

After several minutes, she said, "You hurt me, you know." She waited, but all he did was grip the Bible tightly. The tart smell of diesel blew from the air conditioner vents as they passed a tractor trailer rig loaded with soybeans. "It ain't right what you done. I said no. I said I just wanted a ride home from town. You're a filthy man."

Without looking the preacher swung his right arm, striking her in the mouth with the back of the Bible.

"You're the goddamn devil in this car," she yelled, reaching up to feel her bottom lip swelling. She ran her tongue along the inside of her lip and tasted the sweet, metallic blood. "What you done was wrong, and beating on me now don't make it right any more than the way you put that belt across my ass did. I bet that's the only way you get excited, ain't it."

He jerked his head around to look at her, his eyes swollen and red and his look so fierce she felt her breath catch in her throat like dust.

"God will strike you down, you evil little slut. Don't you use the Lord's name in vain in my car. You're the devil's temptress that made this happen."

"I didn't want that shit you done," she said, lowering her voice. "I told you no. I never said nothing but no."

Charisma stared ahead, saying nothing for a long time. The

car slowed. She looked down at the preacher's brightly polished black wing tips. Expensive shoes. Not like her dirty white tennis shoes from Dollar General. Or her boyfriend's scuffed boots that he'd worn every day since they met.

"I'm stopping right now, and you can get your slutty little self out of my car."

"I wouldn't do that if I was you. I know who you are, preacher. I recognize your voice from the radio. Heard you since I was a kid. And I got your tag number right up here," she said softly, pointing to her temple. "I don't think you want people to know what you done to me. How you hurt me. All I wanted was a ride."

Out the side window the sunset formed long red streaks above the flat Mississippi Delta horizon. She could not ignore its beauty, preacher or not. Her daddy had made sure of that before he died. Every Sunday after church, during the harvest season, he'd take her driving down the parched dirt roads between the cotton fields he called God's back forty. The radio of some Memphis station would be turned down low as background while her daddy pointed out the fields he'd worked.

The stubby bean fields out her window today had been harvested. A foamy sea of cotton tops ran for thousands of acres on both sides of the road, ready for the picker. She wondered if her daddy had cut these very fields before his truck flipped over that early morning, leaving her with no daddy when she was only thirteen.

She saw the jaw muscles working on the preacher's face when he looked over at her. She stared at him as his eyes scanned from her long blond hair, down the front of her tight tee-shirt and to her thighs, only half covered by the blue-jean skirt. Blood rushed to her face as his gaze lingered on her long dirty fingernails. She closed her fists, so her nails didn't show.

"You ain't the first man to force me," she said. "That don't make it alright. You got to make it right."

After another minute of silence, he asked, "What do you mean make it right?"

"I don't know." She hesitated. "I got a baby at home, and you're a man of the cloth. Why don't you make sure my baby's got food on the table?"

****

The tires roared like a distant crowd at a high school football game as the preacher turned sharply into the diner's gravel parking lot. She jerked the door open and stepped out, slamming the door behind her. The tires spun gravel backwards for a dozen feet as the car sped out onto Highway 61.

She walked slowly into the 61 Diner after watching the car disappear north. The smell of cigarettes and brewing coffee filled the room. She sat at the first booth. Greasy dishes, wadded napkins and tiny crusts from something fried littered the red Formica table. She shoved aside a plate smeared with ketchup. The seat felt warm from a large woman in tight black stretch pants, now standing in line to pay.

Charisma leaned forward with her elbows on the table and put her face in her hands. Within seconds, the young man whose trailer she'd shared for nearly a year slid into the booth across from her and pushed back long greasy locks of blond hair from his face. "How much did you get, Char?" he asked in a whisper, looking around.

"It's four hundred dollars, but I got to have some of it for groceries and formula. You can't be spending it all on your damn Camaro."

To Be Loved in Skyline

I watched from Duane's Chevy truck and filed a nail I'd broken locking the door at Dr. Johnson's clinic. Duane grabbed the dried armadillo carcass by the tail and slung it to the side of the road. Its stiff little arms stuck up in the air and reminded me of a Pentecostal prayer meeting. Duane sniffed his fingers, wiping them on his blue jeans as he walked back to the truck. He tossed the croaker sack half full of aluminum cans into the back and dug around in a cardboard box until he found a Pabst can. He walked back to the armadillo and put the can in the animal's grasp like it was lying there drunk.

Duane was the man the *Scottsboro Daily Sentinel* called the "Drunk Armadillo Man" and I was the only one who knew. Sweat dripped off Duane's nose when he leaned out the window to take a picture.

"How many is that?" I asked. I wiped up a few drops of beer that had spilled on the front of my white nurse's uniform when Duane had floored it and made his truck tires scratch up rocks on the roadside.

"Seventeen since Saturday," Duane said, as he spit out the window. "But I don't have no more Pabst cans. We got any Pabst at home?"

"Yeah, I bought a eighteen pack yesterday when I got groceries."

We rode along for ten minutes without either one of us making a peep, which was fine with me. My thoughts were somewhere else. When we got to the intersection of Highway 146 to head up the mountain to Skyline, Duane pulled the truck off the road in front of the stop sign and hopped out. He reached into the back for the sack and started picking up beer cans people had thrown out over the weekend.

Duane worked hard all the time. Two or three mornings a week he'd cut and split a cord of firewood. In the afternoons he'd park his truck on side of Highway 72 and sell the wood. Then he'd pick up cans on the way home and make his drunk armadillos. It didn't bother me that he had a bad temper sometimes. I knew it was just because he had so much pressure on him with a teenage son and having to pay off the boat when he had a house note and a truck payment, too.

I was watching Duane hold his shirttail out like an apron and stack cans in it, but I was thinking about Dr. Johnson and how he had sat me up on his desk after everyone had gone home at five. My arms and legs quivered like I'd put my finger in a light socket when he pushed my skirt up and put his face down there. He always did that first and never did get in too big of a hurry, I guess since he knew Duane was always late. I could feel my own face get hot just thinking about what Dr. Johnson had done. I'd had plenty of boyfriends in high school and junior college, but none of them ever did anything like that. Duane would die if he knew. I didn't know if he'd kill me first or Dr. Johnson, or just kick me out.

I opened my door and got out to help pick up cans.

"I'll get this, Sherrie. Don't get your dress dirty. That dry cleaning costs a lot."

Duane was considerate like that. That's one of the things I liked about him. That and his big arms. He was stronger than any man I knew. And he didn't have too many tattoos. He just had the one strand of blue barbed wire around his muscle on his right arm and an armadillo standing up guzzling a beer. But that one was on his back, and nobody could see it.

Duane treated me nicer than anyone I'd ever met, so I didn't care that he was older than me. Thirty-six didn't seem so old anyway, and I'd dated a couple of men older than that. I'm way more mature than other girls my age anyway, since I graduated high school early and left out from home two years ago on my eighteenth birthday to put myself through junior college.

I leaned against the truck and lit a Marlboro Mild Menthol while he finished kicking through the two-foot tall weeds. I wondered if I'd have to cook supper if Dr. Johnson split up with his wife and married me. I knew it wasn't right to be thinking about marrying someone else while I was Duane's girl, but just for fun it wouldn't hurt to dream about being a doctor's wife. I bet Sunday dinner at the Country Club is a lot better than a crock pot roast floating around in the juice with potatoes and carrots. I looked at my watch and saw it was past six. "Duane, we better get going. Duane Jr.'ll be home from football practice soon."

Duane Jr. was sort of my stepson. Which was kind of funny. The thought had already crossed my mind that when he had his birthday in January I'd only be a year older than him.

"That's all right," Duane said. "I just need to get these few cans and maybe the ones up at the Skyline grocery dumpster, and then we can go home. This load's about big enough to drive down to Scottsboro. What are we having for supper?"

****

Duane Jr. borrowed Duane's truck keys and hit the back door as soon as he ate. He didn't even wait for a bowl of ice cream. I'd finished drying the dishes and was standing at the sink folding the dishrag when I felt Duane's big hands slide around my waist. He put his chin on my shoulder. Then he kissed my neck, and I felt his right hand snake down between my legs. I liked him touching me, but my first thought was I hope he washed his hands good after he handled that armadillo.

"Duane, what are you doing?" I turned around and put my hands on his shoulders.

"What do you think I'm doing?" He had that big smile that I didn't think any woman could say no to. My Momma kept warning me that he'd use that little-boy grin and his smooth talk to get me to do whatever he wanted. I think she was just jealous because they were almost the same age and he didn't care much for her. I know she was right about men saying whatever, just to get in my pants. Plenty of men were like that. But it wasn't like that with Duane.

"Jr. might come back home."

"He's gone until 10:30, when Cindy's daddy makes him leave. We got plenty of time."

"Give me a minute." I pushed Duane back and headed to the bathroom. I at least had to clean up with a washcloth from earlier.

****

I planned to call him Rayford, but when I closed the door behind me and turned around, all I could say was "Dr. Johnson." I'd practiced saying Rayford in my mind a hundred times that day, but when he looked me right in the eye I just couldn't say his name out loud.

He'd been watching me from where he sat behind his computer, with the same smile Duane had when he looked at me the night before. "Is everyone gone?"

"Yes sir," I said, feeling the blood rush to my face again, calling him sir, but the words just came out that way with him being a doctor.

He looked so handsome as he stood up in his pressed black slacks and long white coat and motioned me over to him. He pushed the files back from the middle of his desk. I knew he wanted me to sit up there. I did. I never had been able to say no to him.

He pulled his chair up right between my legs and pushed my feet up to rest on the chair arms. I leaned my head back on the cool leather desktop and closed my eyes while he held my panties over to the side and did what he wanted. I wanted it, too, but I was glad I didn't have to say so.

I peeked out the front window from behind the blinds. Duane was parked over at the far edge of the parking lot where the truck got the little bit of shade from the tall pine tree beside the clinic. The weather was still hot to be so far into September, and I knew he had the truck running with the air on high. I saw him blow smoke out through the opening at the top of the window. I locked the front door and slid the key into my purse. Dr. Johnson would leave out the side door as soon as we drove off.

Two empty Pabst cans lay on the seat next to the Polaroid camera and a new pack of film. Duane was drinking his third beer. He handed me a can from the Little Igloo on the seat. I popped the top as we drove off and pressed the button to lower the window to air out the smoke and stale beer smell. The drive was fifteen miles from the clinic in Gurley back to where we lived in Skyline.

"I seen two armadillos over on Highway 35 this morning," Duane said. "We can go home that way. With a little luck we can put out this whole six pack before supper."

Duane never told me how long he'd been making drunk armadillos. I wanted to ask Becky, his second wife, who was my good friend before she split up with Duane. But she wouldn't talk to me anymore. I tried telling her I didn't have anything to do with Duane while she was married to him, but she didn't believe me. It was mostly true. I only was with him a time or two when they were married, and I knew for a fact they were almost broke up by then. Heather had told me somebody saw Becky with Jimmy Whitehead down at Lake Guntersville drinking beer at the sandbar. Becky had already moved back to her mother's trailer in Paint Rock when Duane and I hooked up. She shouldn't still be mad at me.

On the way home Duane stopped four times to make drunk armadillos. Supper and anything else could wait, but those armadillos were going to get their beer. At one place, there were three of the little critters belly up together. He said they ran in packs and when a car hit one the other ones would go check on it and get hit too. Duane was sort of an expert on armadillos. He propped all three with their backs up against the stop sign and gave each one a beer.

"They look like real party animals, don't they," Duane said. He thought that was the funniest thing ever.

****

I didn't feel too good the next morning. Which was odd, since I only had a few beers the night before. But I felt better by lunchtime. Heather and I went to Hardee's for lunch. All the way there and back, she never shut up asking me about Duane and were we going to get married and stuff. She'd been my best friend since I was a senior in high school, and even helped me get on at Dr. Johnson's office when I passed my certified nurse's assistant test. Heather was a real LPN. She was just the opposite of Momma, who said I was a fool and ought to get my own place. Momma had got on my last nerve, and I was ready to scream if she said that thing about not buying the cow because of the free milk again.

I told Heather that Duane said we needed to wait until he got hired back on at Sherman Concrete and built back up his savings to think about getting married. He'd worked at the plant for a long time driving one of those white cement trucks until they lost the contract for the four-lane highway and he got laid off.

Momma said Duane was just using me, but I knew he loved me. He might not be the type to say it, but I could tell because he treated me so good. He said he was going to get me a Mustang when Junior moved out. And the night before, after we had some loving, he held me tight and fell asleep with my head on his shoulder. I felt really safe snuggled up against him. I just wish I hadn't started thinking about Dr. Johnson right then.

I didn't know what Momma would say about me and Dr. Johnson, but I thought she might be proud a real doctor had such an interest in me. Dr. Johnson told me I was beautiful and had a lovely soul. I once asked Duane if I was beautiful, and he said I was and that I had the prettiest long blonde hair. But he never said anything about my soul being lovely.

I'd noticed on the scales before breakfast earlier that morning that I'd gained two pounds. As I laid there on Duane's arm way past midnight, I thought about maybe going back to junior college to be an LPN, and I hoped I would start my period soon. Dr. Johnson says that a LPN can make three thousand dollars more than a certified nurse's assistant.

After lunch, Heather and I took our smoke break out back of the clinic at the wooden picnic table under the big oak tree. She read "Dear Abby" to me about some woman who wanted to know if it was all right to tell her husband's daddy not to smack his food at the table and ruin Thanksgiving for everyone. Then Heather flipped through the rest of the paper, when all of a sudden she busted out laughing.

"What are you laughing about?'

"That Drunk Armadillo Man. Have you heard of him?"

I'd promised Duane I could keep a secret. "Yeah. I heard of him. He was in the Scottsboro paper and people been talking about him."

"Look at this picture," she'd said, turning the newspaper toward me. A color photograph covered a fourth of the page with an armadillo on his back holding a Pabst can. I recognized the scene from the Curves Ahead road sign in the background and knew the exact location on Highway 146 coming down the mountain from Skyline.

****

I handed Duane the *Huntsville Times* that Heather had given me. He stared at the picture for a long time, holding the page with both hands. Then he got a big grin. "Damn, I'm going to be famous. Look at that."

I was thinking nobody knows who gives the armadillos a beer, so how are you famous? But I didn't say that.

"Why are you doing the armadillos?"

Duane turned red in the face, and I saw him ball up his fist, but he didn't say a word. I didn't mean there was anything wrong with the armadillos, but I knew not to say anything else. He shook his head and looked at me like I must be dumb as a stump, but he didn't say anything. Finally, he walked over to the big kitchen drawer and rummaged around until he found scissors and Scotch tape. He cut out the news article and taped it up on the refrigerator door between the pizza coupons and a picture of six of us standing behind a eight-foot tall pyramid of beer cans we made down at the sandbar when we camped all weekend. That night in the kitchen was the first time Duane wasn't sweet to me.

****

The next day was Saturday. Duane got up at first light. A guy named Earl something or other had called the night before and said the crappie were biting on Lake Guntersville. The three of us were to meet at seven o'clock down at Goose Pond Colony boat landing. Duane was outside loading up the Bass Tracker when I brought him a cup of black coffee.

Duane put down the cane pole he had been rigging up with new line and kissed me on the forehead. "Good morning, Sunshine."

I smiled, but inside I didn't feel like putting on. "How'd you feel if I didn't go with you today?" The way I felt, I knew riding in the boat would be about as much fun as getting a root canal from a plumber. The sun through the pines was pretty, all streaky and red, and it was nice and cool outside right then, but I knew it'd be hot as Hades on the seat of that metal boat when the sun got on up. Hitting all those waves would have me chumming in no time.

"It's all right with me. What are you going to do?"

"I'll just be here cleaning up the house a little. I might call

Heather to come over and ride me down to the Unclaimed Baggage Store. I want to find a coat to wear to work when it turns cold." What I really needed was to tell her that the little strip had a plus that turned pink this morning.

****

All day at work on Monday I practiced what to say to Dr. Johnson. As soon as the other girls were out the front door he hung up a chart he was studying and walked over to where I was bent over putting files away. I kept my head down. He stood behind me and put his hands on my hips and pressed himself into me. I could feel he was getting stirred. I stood up and put a hand on his chest. "The door isn't locked."

He walked over and flipped the dead bolt, then walked back and stood just inches in front of me. I leaned back into the counter.

He put out a hand to the side of my face, rubbing down to my neck. He was so gentle I felt a lump in my throat. His other hand came up to my breast, and he stood there with his palm just touching me tenderly through my white blouse. He looked me right in the eye. "You look so sexy in that tight skirt."

I felt my face burning. No one could make me feel as pretty as he did. I looked down. This wasn't like the first time, when I wasn't very sure about going with a doctor and tried to push his hands away—I knew now I wanted him to go ahead with what he was doing. But I also knew if I didn't say what I had to say right off I might not be able to. "I got to tell you something, Rayford."

He kept circling my nipple with his palm, and I had to look down when I talked.

"I'm pregnant."

His left hand dropped from my breast, and the one that had been on my neck moved down and gripped my shoulder tight enough to hurt a little. "What? Are you sure?"

"I'm pretty sure."

Instead of hugging me the way I'd expected, he let go of my arm and turned around with his back to me. He put both hands on the counter and leaned over with his head down. He wouldn't look at me. I just stood there with my arms folded across my chest and bit the side of my mouth to keep my chin from quivering.

"So now I'm Rayford," he said without looking around at me.

This wasn't the scene I had in my mind when I practiced what to say. I guess I expected him to say we had to get married or something like that.

Instead, he just asked, "How far along are you?"

I couldn't think of how that mattered, but I answered him. "Three weeks late."

"Sherrie, there are a lot of ways to look at this situation."

I didn't like him calling my baby a situation, but he kept talking, and I couldn't think of a thing to say.

"You're not ready to have a child. You don't have to, you know."

I heard gravel crunch under car tires turning in to the parking lot. I walked over to the window and looked through the little white plastic blinds. Duane was early. Of all the days to be early for the first time, he had to pick today.

"I got to go," I said, swallowing hard. I grabbed my purse. I dried my eyes with my sleeve before I opened the door.

"Sherrie, have you told Duane? I'm sure this is his baby, you know."

I turned around, holding my purse against my chest. "I got to go."

"Can we talk tomorrow? Promise me? You're not going to tell him about me are you?"

I nodded, but I didn't promise. I went out the door and locked it behind me.

****

That evening Duane and Duane Jr. and I had a good supper of fried chicken I cut up from a whole fryer myself. It had cooled off some, so we ate at the picnic table he had built out of two by fours in the back yard. We stayed outside until dark drinking Pabst, while Duane tried to fix the wires on his boat trailer so the lights would work. He pumped his fist when he finally got the one on the left side to stay on. I thought this might be a good night to tell him about our baby.

I decided to wait until bedtime to say anything to Duane. After I thought some, I knew this baby must be his. Dr. Johnson was a doctor, and he should know about things like this.

We watched the news on television. Duane had started watching all the time now, ever since that article came out in the Huntsville newspaper with a color picture of one of his armadillos.

"You're not really famous until they put you on TV," Duane had said one day.

So now we watched the news at ten every single night before bed. That night they just talked about the new tire facto-ry coming to Huntsville and how dry the weather still was in North Alabama. There wasn't anything about armadillos.

We were in bed with the lights off, but I could see from the streetlight that stayed on out back at the shed. Duane was finishing his bedtime cigarette and blowing smoke up toward the ceiling through the little shafts of blue light that came through the bamboo blinds.

"Duane?"

"Yeah?"

"I think we're going to have a baby."

I guess what happened shouldn't have surprised me. Just like Dr. Johnson, Duane didn't say anything at first. I wondered if silence was how men always reacted to hearing they were having a baby.

"I thought you was on the pill." His voice sounded like it was from some kind of horror movie when he hissed the words at me.

"I am, well, I was. But that weekend we camped down at the sandbar at the Fourth of July I forgot to take my pills with me. I took three extra pills when we got back, but I guess taking four all at once didn't work."

Duane just lay there not talking, taking such big breaths I could hear the air whistle through his teeth. Then he sat up and leaned over me. His hands gripped my arms and pressed me into the mattress. "Did you get pregnant to trap me? No woman is going to trap me, you know."

"I wasn't trying to have a baby."

"I already got a son, and I'm not ready to start over with a crying baby now that I about got him out of the house. All you girls think about is having a damn baby."

I shook my head and gritted my teeth to keep from crying, while I tried to push him off me. "I said I wasn't trying to have a baby, didn't you hear me?"

"You ain't even been here long enough for me to get you

pregnant, you little slut." The words hit me in the face like a load of buckshot, then I got the other barrel when the back of his hand smacked me in the mouth. I didn't fight back. It was my fault for springing it on him like that.

Duane stood up and put his jeans on and stomped out. As I stared up at the ceiling licking the blood off my swollen lips, I heard the truck crank up. The words had hurt my feelings more than his old thick hand could ever hurt. But I didn't cry. That wasn't the first time I'd got hit.

****

I looked out the window over Momma's sink. Red and gold leaves floated down in a breeze and covered up the grass in the side yard where my rusty swing set had stood for over ten years. I wondered if we could get new seats made and paint the bars up like new.

I helped Momma clear the breakfast dishes off the table and stacked them one-by-one in her new dishwasher. It felt funny reaching so far over to pick up dishes from the counter. "Momma, I'm proud you got you a dishwasher put in. It's real nice."

"Yeah, I'm trying to fix up the place special. That baby needs a good home." I was a little surprised at how kind Momma had been. I'd been living with her for nearly three months, and we hadn't had an argument since the first week. I looked at her for a minute while she folded towels out of the dryer. Maybe I had been wrong about her being selfish and wanting to run my life, which was why I'd left her house the day I turned eighteen and not come back for two years, until now. We had yelled at each other out on the front porch that morning while I threw clothes into Heather's back seat. I felt real bad for having said back then I hated her.

"Momma, do you think I should go ahead and enroll at the junior college to finish those last three courses? I want to get my LPN and find a new job. I just know this baby is a girl, so I'm going to need to make some money for her to have nice things. Girls need nice things so they can grow up special."

Momma pulled the last towels out and closed the dryer. "We'll see, Sherrie. Don't worry about that for now. We'll fix this place up and get that little girl whatever she needs. Don't you worry about that none."

I looked down at my stomach and slipped my hand between the front buttons of my yellow sun dress to feel the baby move. "We have to take extra care of Baby Girl. I love her so much already. When I hold my hand on my belly like this I can feel her there loving me. I can tell she's going to be special. I have big plans for her."

Somehow Momma had enough money for us. I'd go back to work after the baby came, but it felt good to have Momma taking care of me right now. I decided not to worry about it any more. "Momma, I love you."

She just smiled at me and went back to folding towels.

The night before, I'd seen Duane on the television. They said he'd called the TV station and told them he was the one making drunk armadillos. They interviewed him sitting on his front porch without his shirt to show off his armadillo tattoo. He was holding up his scrapbook of all the Polaroid pictures he'd taken to prove he was the real Drunk Armadillo Man. He said he was an artist and the world was his palette. I think if he hadn't been trying so hard on his art project we could have worked it out.

He was real handsome, but he should've combed his hair

better. I wish I could've been there to make sure he wore something nicer than his old blue jeans. I didn't tell Momma about seeing Duane on the news. The one big fight Momma and I had when I'd first come home was about why he wasn't supporting me. I'd had to tell her about Dr. Johnson and how maybe it wasn't Duane's fault for sure.

Sometimes I wish I could go back to work with Dr. Johnson. Not so much to see him, I just miss being there. But after Momma went down and talked to Dr. Johnson about my job, she said it was best if I just stay home from the clinic until the baby is born. Dr. Johnson understood. She said we don't have to worry about money because she had some coming in.

"Momma, come here and feel this."

She folded the last pink towel and set the basket near the hall bathroom door. She walked over and put her hand on my stomach and smiled. "I can feel her kicking."

"She's not kicking Momma. Baby Girl's dancing to let me know she's happy."

"I'm sure she is, Sherrie. I feel like dancing with her." Momma had never been so sweet.

The Turkey Hunt

Jack

Henry Jackson Gaines, Jr., who chose to go by Jack, like his father, stepped down from the chrome running board of his Ford F350 onto dew-soaked grass and looked up. "Damn, I miss seeing the stars," he said, head back, mouth open, staring upward. "Stay in the city too long and you forget how many stars there really are. The lights in Birmingham hide the stars even in the clearest night sky."

His fraternal twin brother Charles Johnston Gaines, dubbed CJ by the family before he could even walk, had downed three cups of black coffee during the fifty-minute drive from the city and now stood on the passenger side of the truck peeing. CJ didn't look up as he answered, "Seen one night sky, you've seen'em all."

Jack stared over the truck bed at CJ, unsure what to say to his younger brother. A middle-of-the-night birth had given the twins different birthdays, something Jack used to his advantage growing up.

Jack saw that six years as a Ranger and two tours in Afghanistan had transformed his pudgy, timid brother into a lean and hard man, a quiet pool of confidence reflecting in his eyes. In the few weeks since CJ arrived home after completing his military service, Jack found his brother's demeanor was nothing like the reserved twenty-two year old who'd boarded a bus to join the Army that bright June morning years before. CJ had told Jack little about his military experience, but the easy smile he'd left home with had been lost in some desolate place. Jack knew only that CJ's past year had been spent in the cold Afghan mountains above Khyber Pass on the Pakistan border, doing what he'd described, when asked by their father, only as "Special Ops." Jack dropped the subject of stars.

CJ zipped up his Army camo pants and turned to open the half door to the truck cab. "You hear any birds yet?"

"Nah, I think we're on time, but let's get on down this hollow before light starts breaking." Jack tilted his coffee cup back for a last swallow, shook a few remaining drops to the ground and tossed the cup onto the truck seat.

Jack pulled a camouflaged backpack from the back seat and began rummaging inside, checking off items from his mental list: owl call, mouth call, box call, extra chalk, shells, water bottle, Snickers bar, face mask, gloves, knife, flashlight. He reached into the truck and grabbed a camouflaged Thermos, dropping the container into the backpack.

Jack glanced sideways as CJ slid an age-worn, but immaculately kept, Parker A-1 side-by-side shotgun from its case and ran his fingers slowly down the smooth twin barrels, then leaned the expensive weapon against the rear truck tire. Jack wondered what his father would say about the shotgun stock sitting in the wet grass and the gleaming barrels leaning on the grit of a mud-caked tire. The borrowed weapon was their father's favorite shotgun, with a field scene hand-engraved into the metal receiver and a Fleur de lis carving in the wood stock. Their father had never let Jack hunt with one of his prized guns. It's just a shotgun, Jack told himself. Hell, my Browning would outshoot that fancy gun any day of the week. As he watched his brother, something in the way CJ caressed the shotgun seemed unnatural.

As Jack arranged the items in his pack, he thought about how he loved the preparation and anticipation of the hunt almost as much as the hunt itself. His routine was largely unchanged in the fifteen years since he and CJ had first turkey hunted together when they were barely teens. He thought back to the days they took to the woods on clear summer mornings with BB guns in hand. We were inseparable back then, he thought, swallowing hard as he felt his throat swelling. He pictured the two of them at the backyard picnic table loading their Boy Scout packs with bottles of water, a pocket knife, kitchen matches, an extra pack of BBs. Jack smiled into the morning darkness, remembering how CJ would invariably sneak two foil-wrapped potatoes from their mom, later roasting them in the coals of a twig fire deep in the woods behind the golf course. He'd not thought of that ritual in years.

For an instant, Jack considered telling his brother he was sorry, he never meant to hurt anyone, we were just kids and I was off at college by myself. But Jack couldn't find words that sounded right. The moment passed.

Jack picked up a can of Deep Woods Off and sprayed heavily around his ankles and at his waistline to fend off the chiggers that were so bad every spring. He could taste the foul chemicals in the air, a small price to pay compared to the weeks of itching caused by the unseen little bugs. After clearing his throat, Jack asked, "You ready?" as he handed the spray to CJ.

"If you're waitin' on me, you're backing up," CJ said.

Jack pulled back the breech on his Browning 12-gauge

autoloader and slid a load of sixes into the magazine. He sighed and stared at CJ's back, a hard frown on his face. He almost blurted out that he knew about Donna and CJ, but decided to keep his newfound knowledge quiet. He knew the time would come to bring up the ancient romance between his brother and the woman Jack had later married, but that discussion would be on his own terms, in his own time. All right little brother, he thought, I guess for now I'll just have to kill this turkey to bring you back to earth and remind you this is my turf.

****

CJ

CJ used his callused thumb to shove a reloaded 2≤-inch shell into his 12 gauge. The night before, he'd used his father's equipment to reload the shell with number two shot, along with enough powder to create a high-velocity, lethal load. The larger shot meant fewer pellets, but he preferred extra knock-down power over a few extra pellets that poorer shooters needed.

After dropping shells into both barrels, CJ slammed shut the breech. He smiled, hearing the solid click of the tightly engineered metal-on-metal. He nodded to himself as he weighed the heft and balance of the gun in his left hand. His Special Operations training as a sniper for the 75th Ranger Regiment had taught him to make a weapon so familiar it became an extension of his own arm. If needed, he could take apart the shotgun in the dark amidst a driving rain and put the weapon back together in seconds.

A breeze on his neck made CJ shiver as he started briskly down a path in front of the truck, not bothering to use a flashlight. After nine months in Bosnia and two years in Afghanistan, he'd learned to walk sure-footed in complete dark to avoid enemy snipers who would creep through the rocks around U.S. encampments to ambush a careless soldier.

Walking in darkness under the full moon took him back to his last week in Afghanistan and the shock of coming face-to-face with someone walking the opposite direction with no light. Only inches away, the moonlight revealed the scraggly beard and astonishment in the dark eyes of the young warrior with a sniper rifle over his shoulder. CJ reacted without thinking and thrust his long knife upward under the man's rib cage, ripping the blade forward to sever the heart like he'd practiced so many times with a straw man during his training. It was him or me, CJ told himself again, but the face hovered there in the faint mist of memory, refusing to fade in the month since the incident. The kill was his ninth confirmed, but all the others were at distances of at least two hundred yards. With the others there'd been no gurgling sounds of lungs struggling for air, no rush of hot body fluids over his wrist, nor the coppery smell of fresh human blood.

"With this full moon the gobblers will be up early," CJ said, picking up his pace a little. The bright moon just above the tree-line took him back to the hours he'd spent talking to the man in the moon, leaning motionless against a large boulder at the edge of his most recent mountain camp in Afghanistan, practicing what to say when he saw Donna again. Until his return he'd not spoken to her since her wedding to Jack, the day before he boarded the bus for basic training.

Walking through the knee-high grass and weeds, CJ thought for a moment about the old pair of snake chaps lying in the back of the truck, but remembered how weighty and cumbersome they felt. He heard Jack's pant legs swishing through the grass a few steps behind. Five minutes later CJ stopped. The heavy breathing behind him, as he reached the top of a hill, told him Jack was out of shape. CJ smiled to himself, but said nothing. He thought back to their days in high school when Jack, two inches taller and three steps faster, had been the star quarterback in football with the perfect physique. While CJ struggled for playing time at defensive guard in high school, Jack was starring on the field and winning a scholarship to Auburn. CJ remembered how proud their father had been when they all gathered around the dining room table as Jack sat with Coach Pat Dye to sign a scholarship commitment. He was proud and thrilled too, despite that fact that no colleges came calling for the slow, short brother.

Now CJ was the one with the six-pack abs, arms bulging beneath his shirt and legs as strong as wooden posts, while Jack added a few pounds to his middle and a slight double chin sitting behind his bank desk all day in suburban Irondale on the edge of the city, occasionally writing a loan to a car dealer expanding a showroom or the hairdresser opening her own shop.

CJ looked down on two big draws drained by sparkling, shallow creeks that merged below the point of the hill. He squatted and breathed slowly through his nose. He scanned the opposite hillside with eyes trained to catch the movement of a single leaf. In the still, quiet morning he heard the sigh of water trickling over dead branches in the creek.

Jack walked up beside him, leaned over with his hands on his knees and gulped for air. The sky lightened as pink and orange streaks rose in soft-edged layers behind black silhouettes of trees scrawled above the horizon.

CJ reached into the front pocket of his Mossy Oak Camo vest and slid out an owl call. He put the string around his neck and placed the wooden call to his lips. He blew hard into the call four times, followed by five more calls, repeating in his mind the mantra, "Who cooks for you, who cooks for you all" that helped him imitate the barn owl so hated by turkeys on the roost.

CJ sat in silence for ten minutes as Jack's breathing returned to normal. He listened to the world waking up around them. The familiar bird songs of morning created a stark contrast to the silent arrival of dawn in the desert after nights when he lay on his belly for hours. These missions found him anxious for the sun to rise behind him as he hid himself near an enemy encampment to identify his target, usually the leader of a rebel group or a small Al Quaida cell. He blew the call again.

Several hundred yards east, an owl answered, "Who cooks for you?" Almost immediately two others responded, followed by a faint, but distinct, gobble. Before the first gobble was finished, a second bird thundered down with a gobble that told everyone in the woods that he was Boss Gobbler.

Curling his eyebrows into a question mark, CJ looked at Jack. Jack pointed toward the gobbler's roost. CJ had hunted with Jack enough that words were unnecessary most of the time. A nod, a tilt of the head or a shrug was adequate. The silence between them might last for an hour as they plodded through the woods, though it was never uncomfortable to CJ, or even noticeable for that matter. But the hush today seemed different, deeper, and CJ wondered if his brother had his own demons to argue with as the turkey hunt pulled them along an unfamiliar road.

CJ nodded agreement at the bird's location, rose to his feet and started off at a trot. The two men half-walked, half-ran down the hill, jumping the three-foot wide creek at the bottom and continuing each on his own path up the other side of the gully.

Limbs of young sweet gums still wet from the humid night air slapped their cheeks. They stopped some two hundred yards from their original spot and listened. Nothing. Two minutes passed. Still nothing.

The sweet fragrance of early spring wildflowers hung thick in the air, reminding CJ how Donna's perfume had surrounded him like fog as she hugged him that day he arrived home on the afternoon flight from Atlanta. He'd tried to prepare himself to see her, but he found few words to say when he saw her standing there between his father and Jack, holding Jack's hand as they waited to pick him up. When CJ hugged her the feel of the firm muscles along her spine and the tuck of her waist were painfully familiar. Her touch made the memories of their long walks on the golf course at sunset that last spring he was home come fluttering to the surface. He'd long ago forgiven her for leaving him and going back to Jack when Jack returned from college. But for a moment his anger toward Jack boiled up in his stomach as he missed her touch. CJ still couldn't understand how Donna had so casually dropped him, when he'd been the one there for her while Jack was off dating other girls at school and never even calling. He didn't doubt the truth of Jack's teenage bragging of conquests with girls at Auburn. A flock of blackbirds swirled into the trees above CJ, lighted for a moment, then flew as one into the sunlight, sounding like rustling paper and disappearing as suddenly as they had come.

CJ watched Jack hold up his owl call and look at him with a shrug. CJ nodded. Jack started the familiar "who cooks for you" owl-calling routine, but before he finished, the boss gobbler answered with a triple gobble.

CJ picked up his father's shotgun and eased quietly up the

ridge to peer over the hill. The sky was filling with yellow light, and the woods around him were now fully awake. His pants legs from the knees down were soaked through from the moisture on the weeds, and tiny black seeds from wild grasses stuck to his Army boots and pants legs. A squirrel darted in front of him and clutched the side of a tree twenty yards ahead staring at the intruder, barking his alarm to the world.

The air rumbled as the turkey gobbled again. Although the thick hardwood forest made distances hard to judge, CJ knew the bird was close now. It's almost time, he thought. Are you ready?

CJ moved forward another forty yards. He stopped to listen and leaned the gun against a tree as he squatted to scan ahead with his binoculars.

"CJ, don't you think we're close enough?" Jack asked, walking up behind him. Jack had his mouth open, sucking in as much air as he could without making noise. CJ enjoyed the workout his brother was getting, but he didn't want to let the turkey see them from its high vantage point, roosted somewhere in the tall oaks, or one of the scattered forty-year-old pines that stood like smooth wooden towers in contrast to the gnarly hardwoods. "All right, let's set up here. Take that tree up there," CJ said quietly, pointing. "That white oak will hide your outline. I'll set up behind you and call."

Like his brother, CJ sat against a large tree to hide his silhouette, gun propped across his knees pointing in the direction of the turkey to minimize any movement needed to get off a shot. He would be facing the sun, which went against his training, but there was too much risk in trying to circle around the bird now.

CJ slid his box call out of his pocket, found a small piece of chalk and rubbed it over the smooth surface of the wooden striker. He moved the thin piece of wood gently across the walls of the box to imitate the soft cluck-cluck-cluck sounds of a roosted hen.

In response, three gobbles shook the ground, all from the same turkey. CJ waited two minutes and repeated his soft hen calls. Two more gobbles. He placed the call beside his leg. Now the hunt became a waiting game.

CJ sighted down the barrel of the shotgun resting on his knee toward the side of his brother's head resting against a big red oak. "Bang," he said, his finger light on the trigger.

Five minutes later the gobbler let them know it was still interested, rattling the woods with two gobbles, followed moments later by three gobbles.

CJ watched as Jack turned his head to look back over his shoulder. CJ knew Jack might be able to see a big smile on his face, even through the thin camo face net. But he knew Jack would have no idea why he was really smiling.

****

Jack

Nothing is more exciting than being this close to a hot turkey, Jack thought. He could feel his heart's doubletime march in rhythm with his breathing. When the time comes, he'd be quickest with the shot, just like the old days. Sweat ran into his ears, but he dared not move. Any minute he would hear the turkey drumming the ground to signal the hen he was hers, and soon the big bird would walk over the hill for its last time. Jack had a vision of twelve-inch beard, maybe even a double beard, and spurs two inches long. His only goal was to be the one showing the plump gobbler and trophy beard to his father and Donna.

After another half hour, he fought the urge to stretch. His leg and back muscles tightened from sitting absolutely still, and he wondered if CJ, with his military conditioning, felt the same way. He'd noticed how much easier the walk had been for CJ that morning, and he resolved he'd soon get back in shape. He'd been meaning to get back on the weight machine anyway. And maybe he'd take Donna up on her offer for evening walks on the golf course. Trimming up wouldn't take long if he could just find the time. But today he wouldn't allow himself to move and risk ruining the hunt. The story would be told and retold. Donna would tease him, and he'd have no choice but to laugh along with everyone else. He'd noticed Donna's eyes widen when she first saw CJ walk off the plane. He couldn't ignore how his brother's former soft facial features, slumped shoulders and extra few inches around the middle had been replaced by a strong chin, stiff back and flat stomach.

Jack closed his eyes, wondering how his life could change so much in just the few days since his brother had been home. His bank job seemed to grow unimportant to everyone but him. His work leading the Downtown Revitalization Committee merely busy work. When his dad was around, he seemed obsessed with CJ's opinion about this military strategy in Falujah or that offensive on the northern front, and did CJ think Bush would strike Iran or Syria next to root out terror around the world? More than once Donna had mentioned how handsome CJ looked and how he'd come back very different. Jack found himself thinking again of Donna and CJ together, after Jack had mostly ignored her during his years away at college. Two nights before, after another of Donna's comments about CJ's new good looks, he'd shouted at her for the first time ever. At some point in the screaming match that followed Donna blurted that, yes, she and CJ had been more than friends. Jack had ceased yelling and just stood there quietly as the words sunk in, giving life to suspicions that hadn't bothered him in years.

A breeze swept the leaves around Jack's feet, making him open his eyes to scan the woods for movement. Jack knew a silent gobbler could be strutting just over the hill, its feathers puffed up and wings dusting the ground, or easing quietly down the draw in search of the lonesome hens he and CJ were imitating with their calls. He decided not to risk the hand movement required to operate the box call. Slowly, shifting his hand to his mouth, he put a diaphragm call between his teeth and sat there soaking the plastic. He tried a series of four soft yelps. His patience was rewarded when the gobbler filled the air with another triple gobble. The bird was no closer, but hadn't moved away either.

After another 15 minutes, Jack knew the gobbler wasn't coming in. Sometimes a gobbler simply wouldn't cross a creek, or go down a hill, to reach a hen. The bird would sit there for hours gobbling, but come no closer. He placed his calls in his shirt pocket and crawled slowly back to CJ.

"He's hung up," Jack whispered.

"If you're that impatient, Junior, we can ease up here and see what's over this hill."

Jack took a deep breath, but said nothing. CJ called him Junior just to piss him off, and Jack didn't want to give his brother satisfaction by responding. Although Jack was only minutes older, he'd gotten their father's name. He played the part of big brother as kids and his being taller always made people assume he was the older brother.

Jack crouched beside CJ and made his way up the hill, pushing branches aside and stepping over dried sticks to avoid giving away their location. As he surveyed the woods ahead, the gobbler offered a single gobble. The bird sounded just beyond the next hill.

Jack crept down an embankment, waded a stream and started up the other side. CJ was five feet to his left. On hands and knees the two made their way through underbrush and briars, aiming for an opening just below the crest of the hill. A stand of tall, straight poplars and thick-limbed shagbark hickory trees created a canopy that had killed most of the undergrowth.

Before reaching the opening in the woods, Jack's shirt had soaked through in the humidity. He said nothing and moved as quietly as possible, knowing they were close and fearing the turkey would spot them if they made a sound. In his years of hunting, he'd often experienced the explosion of flight from a tom turkey that had spotted him. He was determined not to be the one to screw up. They might not harvest the turkey, but the blame wouldn't be on him. He pictured the family seated around the large formal dining table Donna would have prepared, he at the end near the window, Donna to his right where she always sat. The topic would be the hunt, and Dad would lead the discussion. Who saw the turkey first? Who called best? You should've waited on him instead of scaring him away like that.

CJ's voice brought him back to the moment. "Why don't you set up in front. I'll be back here to the side." Jack stared for a moment without replying, then placed himself with his back to a wide white oak tree.

CJ

CJ held his hand beside his mouth to muffle the sound and made four short hen clucks on the mouth call. From just over the hill CJ heard a desperate series of gobbles unlike anything he'd ever heard. He felt his pulse speed up as he held his shotgun to his shoulder, cheek pushed hard into the stock at ready. This is it, he thought, as he watched the woods beyond his brother's outline.

CJ thought his calling sounded just right, even though he'd been away from hunting—at least for sport—for years. Despite all the ways a turkey could make a hunter doubt his skills, this time CJ knew he'd succeed. He heard a sound and caught movement in the leaves just to his left side. His breath caught in his throat as he saw the thick snake only two feet away, sliding side-to-side toward his outstretched legs, its tongue flicking at his boots.

For a moment he'd hoped it was a gray rat snake, but when his movement caused the snake to raise its head and open its mouth, he saw the vertical slits of the eyes. The cream and black lines on the wide pointed head and the diamond designs along its broad back confirmed his fear. He didn't need to hear the rattles clicking their warning. The Eastern Diamondback Rattler's open mouth showed inch-long fangs. CJ carefully moved his shotgun barrel toward the snake. The snake lunged and struck the cold steel. CJ pressed down with the barrel and pinned the snake's head on the ground. He reached over and gripped the snake just behind its head. The snake wriggled furiously in his hand. Its glistening mouth was open, dripping fangs extended, but CJ only gripped tighter as he slid his Ranger knife from his boot with his left hand and cleanly severed the head in one

34

stroke, kicking it away from where he sat. The snake continued to twist in his hand. He tossed the squirming body behind him and wiped the blood off the back of his hand onto his pants leg. He looked over and knew that Jack had seen nothing.

CJ raised the shotgun and clucked a single time on his mouth call, and again the turkey cut loose with a string of gobbles. Double gobbles followed by triple gobbles. The turkey's pleading was non-stop. Lovesick. Relentless.

As the minutes passed, CJ had to raise his knees to hold the heavy gun, but he dared not lower the barrel and risk missing the shot. He slowly swung his aim left until he could see Jack's head behind the tiny bead sight. Bang, he mouthed again.

Twenty minutes later, CJ lowered his shotgun, puzzled, after he saw Jack do the same. Had they misjudged the distance? What had made this gobbler hang up so badly? Ten minutes more, he told himself. You've waited six years. Be patient.

Jack

Jack had been listening for the turkey, but he couldn't get last night out of his mind. Donna had rolled over and pressed her breasts into his back, her nipples already hard, and slid her hand between his legs. He'd first willed himself to respond, but after a moment pushed her hand away. He couldn't force Donna's revelation about CJ out of his head. "I'm too tired," he said, realizing even as he was saying the words that he didn't have the resolve even to fake being tired. He kept thinking her excitement was about CJ, not him. She'd practically admitted so when she'd gotten mad after he pushed her hand away. "I bet CJ wouldn't have said he was too tired," she said, rolling over with her back to him and pulling the covers tightly around her. Her words kept replaying in his head as he lay there not sleeping, staring up at the faint image of the slowly turning ceiling fan. The harder he tried to forget, the more the words kept circling through his mind like song lyrics on an endless loop. The loop kept playing all morning.

Finally Jack's patience evaporated like the sweat on his arms. He looked at his watch. Ten forty-five. They'd been chasing this turkey for four hours. Enough is enough. He lowered himself onto his stomach and began slowly, painstakingly crawling forward. Minutes passed. He inched forward. The turkey kept gobbling. Jack kept crabbing ahead. He neared the high point of the hill, taking ten minutes to cover just twenty-five yards. As he raised his head to peer over the hill, he heard the gobble that was now all too familiar as his eyes locked onto the beautiful bird in full strut, chest puffed up, and dusting the ground with outstretched wings.

The bird was every bit the majestic tom that Jack had hoped for. Now he would assume the honored role of story-teller, the center of the family's attention around the dinner table that night.

But this was one turkey Jack wouldn't harvest. He closed his eyes for a few seconds in disbelief, then rolled onto his back. "This is perfect ending to a perfectly ridiculous day," he thought. At first he chuckled as he put his hand over his mouth, and finally he erupted with rousing laughter that echoed through the woods.

CJ

CJ propped his shotgun on his knee, looking over the barrel. If you just stand up maybe our little ballet can all be over Junior.

Accidents happen all the time while turkey hunting. Through his brother's laughter the turkey kept gobbling.

CJ rose, baffled by Jack's amusement, and removed his camo mask. As he stood, he reached back for the snake and gripped the thick middle, feeling it squirm as if still alive. Walking toward Jack, he spotted the huge gobbler strutting thirty-five yards ahead, a trophy beard dragging the ground, with Jack directly between them. The gobbler's head showed a brilliant red in the morning sunlight. CJ quickly raised the Parker with one hand, watching Jack's eyes grow wide and his entire body become rigid as he looked into the open ends of the barrels pointed his direction. CJ saw Jack's eyes lock onto his, held there by some invisible chain. He saw the look of fright pass over Jack as if the sun had shifted its orbit, creating a shadow that moved across Jack's face like a veil.

Neither man moved or blinked as time seemed to stop for that instant. Jack's eyes narrowed, and the wrinkles in his forehead relaxed; his tightly pressed lips softened into a smile and CJ noticed Jack nod. CJ squeezed off quick shots using both barrels. Jack went face down into the leaves and dirt, and was still.

Within seconds the woods grew calm as the echo of shots faded. The breeze ceased. Small birds hopped nervously from limb to limb. Shafts of sunlight pierced the dense trees, illuminating specks of dust drifting to the forest floor. At the base of the hill, a bloody turkey quivered and kicked its death dance inside a chicken-wire pen behind a light blue mobile home in a well-kept yard carved into the edge of the lush, green forest bordered by a red clay road.

CJ tossed the snake inches in front of his brother's head, turned his back on the scene and started to the truck.

Hearing leaves rustle, CJ looked back as Jack raised himself on both arms, his cheeks glowing crimson and jaw clenched tight. The veins in his neck bulged. Mildewed, moist leaves stuck to his quivering chin.

"Let's go, Brother," CJ said over his shoulder, his tone becoming gentler, almost matter-of-fact. "I guess I've got my limit." He walked quickly to keep ahead of Jack, allowing the breeze to dry the moisture gathering in his eyes.

The Story of
William B. Greene

William B. Greene was an easy target if you wanted to kid someone, with his hair long and beard scraggly, his skin tan and leathery, like an alligator, I remember thinking. Little did I know that an alligator would be Willie's end. I once kidded him, "Willie your toenails are long enough to gig flounder." Stuff like that. He always laughed as loud as anyone and never seemed offended. We didn't know Willie's full name until after he died, like so many things I'm finding we don't really know about the people we call friends. He was just Willie.

When he did die, his momma said to me on the telephone, after I told her I'd help with the funeral plans, "Tell the undertaker to make sure they cut his hair nice and trim his beard like when he was a Sailor."

Willie in the Navy? Never saw that one coming. None of us knew Willie had a momma or any family at all until she called me up the day after Willie died.

"I got your name from the newspaper article," she said.

"We read books together," I told her, not sure what to say.

I saw her at the funeral, but didn't get to know her until she showed up at the sentencing hearing wearing a big church hat with fake magnolia blossoms to shade her eyes—she kind of squinted the same way Willie did. We sat outside the courthouse on a concrete bench, under a thick oak tree, while she told me how much Willie had loved being a teacher before his nervous breakdown. I'd never have guessed that either. I never saw anything jittery about him. There was something else about a student who killed herself, but I didn't get the details. A few things started making sense, except for Willie being gone.

I only knew Willie for three years, but those were the best three summers of my life. Well, the first two were great anyway. We met on a Sunday at the sand bar when everybody else my age was there drinking beer in their hot boats, the girls all shooting us glances, making sure we noticed them rubbing down with suntan oil. I didn't have a hot boat, only a sixteen foot Army-shit-green flatbottom with a 25-horse Mercury, the green fake grass carpeting ripped up in strips. We used it to haul cases of beer, ice chests and folding chairs. So that day I was cruising with Rocky, whose boat was pimped black with silver flames licking the tinted glass windshield. Black leather seats. A motor so big the bottom of the boat could skip the tops of waves. Rocky was trying to catch the attention of Brieanne, an Ole Miss sophomore who ran hot and cold. Hot when she wanted to ski. Cold when a nicer boat showed up. You know the scene: camping out on an island at the sand bar, chicks trying to tan without strap marks, skiing in the afternoon, drinking under a full moon and no cops. And then there was Willie. The island's one resident.

Actually, we never knew if Willie left the island, though once in awhile I saw his little jon boat had been moved. I asked him a couple of times, but he'd just wink or smile. He was there the first good weekend in March when it got warm enough for us to camp with the makeshift gear we put together. And if you went to the island on a Sunday afternoon in the fall, when everyone had left for college and deserted the island on the weekends for football games and the promise of a drunk and willing date, the latest version of Willie's tent would still be there. I had met Willie in March and knew he was older, though I found out later not as old as he looked. He asked me that day if I liked to read, then slowly untied a bright blue tarp from a rusted chrome shopping cart that held a shit load of paper backs, musty and rippled from the damp.

I'd had my fill of reading the crap they make you read in college, but I didn't tell Willie that. He was sort of like the old granddaddy of everyone down here. Not that he was that old or anything, but he just sort of kept things in order. Most of the time he kept a little off to the side, but not unfriendly like. He just did his own thing, tending his tomato plants and reading, scratching with a pencil in one of his spiral bound notebooks he kept dry in big plastic bins in his tent.

Around the night fire that kept the mosquitoes away, we'd invite Willie over to share a joint and the cold ones we'd iced down between layers of ice and rock salt that made the beer so cold it would form little ice crystals. If some guy drank past his limit and got mean drunk, Willie could crack a joke or tell a story that could stop a fight before it even happened. Some of the girls—Brieanne was one—said Willie was creepy, a freeloader. From what I could tell, mainly what Brieanne understood was money, hygiene, and pects. Willie seriously lacked all three.

That first day, Willie reached into the basket and pulled out *Catcher in the Rye*. "You know this book?" he asked me. Said I couldn't go through life or think I was educated and not read it.

I looked around to see if anyone was listening, ready with

a smart-ass dig if I said the wrong thing. This wasn't the kind of comment I'd ever heard on the river, or outside class for that matter. I was at loss for words. Willie didn't press me to talk, just pushed the book into my hand and pointed a knotty, crooked finger down toward the lawn chair at the edge of the water with a beach umbrella stuck in the sand beside it, half the umbrella's green and blue cloth missing but leaving enough to shade the one chair if you moved around as the day went on. That was the first book I actually read all the way through not because I had to.

After a few weeks that first summer it sort of got to be a routine that I would get a book from Willie and spend some time reading in his favorite lawn chair by the water's edge. *Walden, Catch 22, Leaves of Grass*, anything by John D. MacDonald. Then when nobody else was around Willie would ask me what I thought or what I liked in the books. We'd talk for an hour or two sometimes, especially in the mornings over coffee when we were the only ones up, and I learned stuff from him about why this or that was in a book. Sometimes it seemed like we weren't even talking about the same book. Once, he got so excited when I told him about a book I read at home on my own, he came over and hugged me. He said, "You get it." Which I have to say made me feel good, but still I was looking over his shoulder and hoping no one was looking.

I learned by accident that books make chicks curious. I guess sitting there reading made me appear smart or maybe like I wasn't trying to get laid. Whatever, I was getting more action with much less effort. The chicks saw me reading and wanted to talk, and once I got them talking and maybe threw in a quote from Thoreau or Emerson, the rest was cake.

And here I was again this summer doing the same thing. I'd read some, then drink a couple of Silver Bullets before taking a turn driving or skiing. I drove whenever I could, because some cute girl would ride lookout and flirt. The day of the boat wreck seemed like any other day, up to that point. Willie picked me a book and I wandered down to the chair, where I soon found myself tearing through the pages of *Love in the Ruins*. Well, not actually tearing I guess, but for me it seemed that way once I got hooked into thinking about this cool machine the guy in the book invented and how to look inside someone for how they feel, the same way you look at what they do instead of what they say. I didn't know yet how that story would color a situation for me, but I had fun reading about the South like things had gone to hell. The dude who wrote that book was seriously disturbed. But I enjoyed imagining that maybe what we thought we were seeing wasn't really happening. I felt that way half the time anyway. Just then, Rocky drove his boat up and cut the engine to drift past the girls sitting with their feet in the water. I closed the book and looked down where Brieanne and two friends, Brooke and Amber, were sunning but occasionally glancing my way as they waited for a turn to slalom behind Rocky's boat or to ride on the pontoon that kept cruising by, full of drunks, Lynyrd Skynyrd on the boom box.

"Hey Brieanne, come spot for me," I heard Rocky yell. Like I said, he had a thing for Brieanne and for two summers had tried to get her in the boat every chance he got. After Brieanne climbed over the side and sat down facing backwards, Rocky stood the boat up and roared down the river with some guy I'd never seen, hanging on for his life at the end of the ski rope. The pontoon boat pulled up and Brooke and Amber left too. Amber's real name wasn't Amber. I remembered her from junior high as Aileen Mary something or other, with glasses like Coke bottle bottoms back then, but I don't think she remembered that I had known her pre-Amber, before the blue contacts.

An hour later I looked up and realized I was all alone. The ski boats, jet skis, and a few bass boats going from one honey hole to another seemed to stop all of a sudden. Even in the shade and with my feet in the water, I felt the sweat running down the side of my face. There was no breeze to help. The waves lapped up under my chair for a few seconds before the water calmed to smooth flat, and the whine of the two-stroke engine of the Tracker that had just passed faded and then went silent up the river. Bird whistles and cricket chatter that usually filled the air went silent, and I couldn't remember it ever being this quiet on the river. Where *was* every one? Even Willie, who would usually be leaned against a tree somewhere in the shade, a dog-eared paperback in hand, was nowhere in sight. All I could see was blue sky and a couple of wispy white clouds hovering there motionless, but it was like waking up one otherwise normal morning and wondering what the hell had just gone wrong.

After another couple of minutes, I put the book down and started walking the edge of the sand bar, looking up river. When I reached the narrow end where sand gave way to mud and snagged drift wood, I waded out onto a bank of muscle shells into water about ankle deep and looked beyond the stand of willows. About half a mile up river I could see fifteen or twenty boats all floating close to each other, but it was hard to tell anything about what they were doing. I heard someone splash through the water behind me, and there was Willie, with a huge pair of Marine binoculars from God knows where. He stood there with his eyes pressed into the binoculars, mumbling Oh Jesus, Oh Jesus.

I heard the helicopter drumming the ground as the big red and white machine whirled in low behind a stand of cypress trees before I saw it land in a field close to the bend in the river. Someone was being airlifted, but nobody seemed to be in a hurry. I knew what that meant. Willie grew silent and looked at me with a deep sadness in his eyes, then turned and walked back toward his tent shaking his head and muttering cuss words over and over. He didn't come out for the rest of the day.

Later, people drifted away from the cluster of boats and came back to the island to tell their versions of what had happened. I felt like I was the one that saw it most clearly, but I hadn't even been there to see the blood, or smell the gasoline floating on the water. What I saw, I saw from a distance, no more existent than a dream. Like when you hear that Hurricane Katrina's been made into a movie, or when you see your best friend's picture on MySpace, and he's got his arm around you, and you're both smiling and holding beers. Only then does it hit you that it's real. Sometimes I think you have to back away and look at something sideways out of the corner of your eye to feel like you've really seen it.

Amber had jumped from the pontoon into a ski boat that, after a while, took on some water, so the guy driving started going real fast and told his friend sitting in the back of the boat to take out the drain plug, so the water would flow out. But then the drain plug somehow got lost, and in the confusion the driver panicked and started yelling at the people in the back of the boat more than watching where he was going. So when the ski boat crashed into the pontoon, Amber was ejected and ended up with a broken neck. She had taken off her ski vest because it was messing up her tan—Brieanne told me that part—so she drowned.

At least twenty people told me pieces of the story that day. Many were people I had seen all summer but never saw again, not that summer, not since.

After Amber died most all the girls quit coming to the island. A few guys still came to drink beer, but the skiing stopped. And no one bothered even to bring a radio, so the music stopped too. Then rain hit every weekend for a month. Late summer arrived. For many, time to go back to school. All those rich parents from Memphis with the big summer houses suddenly woke up, I guess, and realized their daughters were in danger. "Hanging with the wrong crowd," I imagined them saying. Willie now spent all of his time in his tent, bent over one of his spiral notebooks with a short pencil in one hand and his pocket knife in the other. He constantly whittled at the pencil to keep his lead sharp while he filled page after page.

****

Things changed. There was the boat wreck, then the next spring the invasion of Eurasian milfoil which was like this alien life form that just took over the water. One weekend there was just a tiny bit of it here and there. The next weekend the deep green strands were everywhere, getting sucked up into the intake systems of the jet skis and totally putting them out of business. And who would want to ski in it? At first it was mostly under the water, but soon leaves and debris got caught in it, and the eddy parts of the river became a green bog. The frogs, turtles, and snakes loved the swampy feel of this bog which had been a flowing river, so a bunch of them moved in around our island too. Some nights, the bullfrog noises were so loud there was no use trying to sleep. And then there was the smell. Not real bad, just sort of a sweet decaying odor like when the wind changes and you get a little whiff of the paper mill right when you are enjoying the honeysuckle blossoms.

The few of us, who hadn't given up on the good times we remembered, sat drinking around the night fire, shooting the shit one Saturday. Though a year had passed, everyone knew we could never make things right again. Eventually everyone drift-ed off except Willie, Rocky and me, leaving the island in their boats one by one as the light faded completely. We sat in silence for a few minutes until we heard a splash in the slough behind the island. We all turned and looked, as if we could see into the black, but nothing big seemed to be moving. Big fish, alligator, beaver—whatever had splashed grew quiet. That's when Willie started going on about alligators, and Rocky went crazy.

"What in hell you mean gators don't care about people?" Rocky yelled. "I seen a picture of a gator with a whole deer in his mouth. That's bigger than a person. And it was from right around here somewhere."

The story about the picture of the gator swimming across the river in broad daylight with a whole deer was true. A game warden took the shot from a helicopter. Someone emailed me the picture, and I'd forwarded it to Rocky, but I didn't know if the photo came from around here. Rocky added that part, just adapting the story without really lying outright, like everyone does when they need to win an argument. I heard the game war-den was in Alabama. Either way, we had plenty of gators right here, and no one questioned that. We saw their orange eyes glowing at night all the time when we shined spotlights from the boats, but there was sort of an unspoken man-law not to do that or speak about the gators around girls. I even saw a big gator at Christmas one year when I was duck hunting behind the island on a sunny day, too warm for December and duck hunting, but we didn't care. Anything was better than a house crammed with family and too much ham. I was standing in four feet of water when I heard something blow, and there the damn thing was, an eight-footer idling ten feet away with just his eyes and nostrils above the water line like he was watching the ducks with my hunting buddy and me. So I knew the gators would come up close, no matter if the temp was below 70 degrees, when they supposedly go off their feeding.

Willie was talking that night about how these two gators would slide up on the sand bar and lay there looking up at the tent. "Like they were hungry," Willie added, after he cut a glance over at me, grinning when Rocky wasn't looking. "Hell, that was probably them making that splash we heard," Willie said, a fake serious look on his face.

The fire popped and a small chunk of glowing ember flew toward Willie, who used his bare foot to push sand over the red coal, so he wouldn't step on it. Willie was nice and you might even say gentle. But for some reason he enjoyed getting Rocky so wound up that his little bald spot would glow red, which was easy ever since Rocky had a bad motorcycle wreck. That's where Rocky got his name, too. He rode that damn bike everywhere and everyone started calling him Crotch Rocket, and then we shortened it to Rocket, then Rocky. What got Rocky really going was when Willie let it slip that he was feeding the creatures fish behind the island. Rocky didn't have much good for Willie, ever since the day Willie had said Rocky's Speedo swim suit made him look like a Southbeach gigolo in wet underwear and Brieanne had laughed at him. The next weekend Rocky had a new suit, a big baggy one down to his knees with palm trees and swirls of foamy breaking blue waves, like surfers wear. Rocky never forgave Willie for the way Brieanne tilted her head back and blasted a belly laugh toward the sky. Not only could she burp like a man, she laughed like one, too. Rocky knew he had no chance with Brieanne after that, and he was different, quieter most of the time. Of course we all already knew he never did have a chance with Brieanne. Especially me. She had made out with me in the water a few times while everyone else was off skiing. Oh, I suppose Willie had seen from somewhere back in the trees or sitting inside his tent, but it was easy to simply act as if he were not there. Brieanne liked playing the blond role, but when it was just us she talked about things like work and the economy and politics, and sounded a lot smarter. I'll never forget that first time she swam up to me, grabbed the back of my head and kissed me so hard my lips hurt. She smiled the biggest smile, like she was saying, I'm full of surprises. In between the four or five times we made out in the water, she acted like it never happened. I knew not to screw up a good thing, so I never said a word to anyone.

"How you know so fucking much about gators?" Rocky asked Willie, picking at the fire with a stick, shooting sparks out in all directions. He sort of spit his words, saliva flying like little wet exclamation points in the light from the fire. Rocky was getting mean drunk like he did more and more since the girls quit coming. He smashed his beer can flat against his head and threw the metal disk into the fire, and then staggered off toward his ice chest that was still in his boat. I guess the metal plate in his skull from the motorcycle wreck didn't hurt as much as we figured.

I had my tent on the island that weekend, but I was thinking about not staying. I'd been on the island for a day and a half, and I thought a shower might feel pretty good. I had my own apartment since graduating in December and didn't mind going home as much now that I didn't have to share a place with two slobs, my former roommates.

When Rocky walked back up the sandbar he had two beers and tossed one to me without asking if I wanted another one. Hauling back only two beers instead of three seemed like his way of choosing sides, like it was Rocky and me against Willie. I did-n't have a side, but the beer in my hand made it easier to decide I didn't really want to take my boat back to the landing in the dark and drive thirty minutes back to town. I finished my beer and decided to go crawl inside my tent, which I always set up about a hundred and fifty yards away, where it was quieter and I could get the shade of a big oak in the afternoons. I had a cot there that slept pretty good, so I left Rocky and Willie sitting on opposite sides of the fire still arguing about alligators and what alligators liked to eat. Willie said frogs and turtles; Rocky insist-ed it was warm meat. I must have had more to drink than usual, because the frogs—obviously not afraid of gators if their croak-ing was any indication—didn't keep me from falling asleep, and I didn't wake up at all until I heard a boat's high-pitched engine whining past the island around daybreak. By the time the crum-pled paper sound of the waves rolling onto the sand bar quit, I was too awake to go back to sleep, so I unzipped the tent and walked out to see about making some coffee. The bullfrogs that filled the slough behind the island were still rattling the trees with a cacophony of frog songs and warnings. And the rotten smell of the dead weeds choking the life from the slough was the worst I could remember.

After I peed in the river, I walked up to what served as our kitchen—it was mostly just a fold-out table holding a three-burner Coleman stove with a couple of frying pans, a coffee pot, and miscellaneous spatulas with dried egg stuck to them and greasy spoons piled up. Something wasn't right. The plastic storage bin we kept there for paper plates and cups was turned over and crushed flat. Little white napkins were blowing down the sand bar like seagulls running on a beach. Behind the kitchen at the edge of the woods, I saw one pole holding Willie's lean-to was knocked down, and his roof was tilted at the wrong angle. Willie wasn't inside. Rocky wasn't anywhere around, and I realized the boat I heard must have been him leaving.

Something had been dragged through the sand toward the little slough behind the island, leaving twin furrows like a plough, so I followed the trench marks through a thin line of willows. I walked almost to the water. About twenty feet across the shallow slough a gator was sitting there with a human body in its jaws. It wasn't chomping down or eating. It sat motionless. The person's head was under the water. Already dead, I could tell. There was nothing to do. I didn't know it was Willie yet. I turned and ran all the way back to my boat, yelling for Willie and Rocky the whole way, even though I knew Rocky was off in his boat.

I found the game warden at the landing, and he said he would come down after calling the sheriff and the other game warden for the county. I noticed Rocky's boat parked next to the landing, but he wasn't around and I couldn't see his truck either. He loved that boat, and seeing it here without him gave me a bad feeling in my stomach.

Eventually the game warden and sheriff got a noose on the gator and got the body out of its jaws when it turned to fight and started rolling around and around. I was standing back on the sandbar with a couple of fishermen who had gathered around to watch. I remember thinking this was too pretty a day, with such a blue sky and all, for someone to die here. But the rotten, decay smell seemed to get worse by the minute. When they called me over to look at the body and see if I knew who it was, I almost fell backwards. Not because it was Willie—I'd sort of expected that by now. It was the duct tape around his legs and mouth that got me. I sat down on the sand. I felt dizzy, one of those moments when you wonder if what you're seeing is real or not.

****

There never was a trial, just a fifteen-minute sentencing hearing after Rocky pleaded guilty in a plea bargain before the trial started. Rocky got sentenced to fifteen years for some kind of charge that wasn't real murder. When they found Rocky at home that same day Willie died, he was sitting on his couch crying. He never tried to run or deny that he had duct taped Willie up and left him beside the water. He said he just wanted to scare Willie and prove that Willie was lying about not being afraid of gators eating a person. I know for a fact Rocky and Willie were both bad drunk when I'd gone to bed that night. Not that drinking makes it all right. Rocky said he went back at sunup to let Willie loose and saw that a gator had dragged him off.

I took Brieanne to the funeral and then she said she had a headache from not eating. I hadn't felt much like eating that morning, so I was hungry too. We stopped at the Waffle House for cheesy eggs and coffee. She surprised me by telling me how sorry she was about Willie and that she had noticed I was probably Willie's best friend. I hadn't thought of it like that.

The next night we ate dinner at Shucker's and then hung

out for beers when the band started. Looking back, there never was a real date, like I asked her out for a movie or a concert. But the next thing I knew she had a toothbrush next to my sink, ten kinds of lotions in the cabinet and pink razors on the side of my bathtub. I think she wants to get married, but I just don't bring up anything like that. We never go down to the sandbar any more, even though I ended up with Rocky's boat. The water grew too full of weeds to ski, and all the old crowd has drifted apart anyway.

****

I'm visiting Rocky in prison today. Brieanne wouldn't come. The two-hour drive up to the prison always brings back memories of Willie. Last weekend I finally visited his mom. She had called two or three times, but I kept putting off going over there. I don't like to get that involved with stuff that's not mine to worry about. And to tell the truth, I didn't much like the way I felt a dull ache when I thought of Willie. I had starting reading Willie's notebooks and found out they were journals of what he thought and saw, and all about the people he met. He drew little sketches of us. Lots of sketches and quotes of things we'd said. Good enough pictures to know who it was, too. I was in a bunch of the journal entries. He wrote that I was the closest friend he had in years, which made me feel worse instead of better. One entry seemed ironic, saying Rocky would have to die young if he wanted his IQ to stay higher than his age, but that there was something about him Willie just had to like. I never told anyone that before. And I sure won't bring that up when Rocky and I sit in the prison lunchroom to talk.

During my visit with Willie's mom, she offered me three boxes of books that had been Willie's favorites. The cartons were stacked in a bedroom that had been made into an office she said was his. The room was a shrine. There were all sorts of certificates and framed awards on the wall, including his diploma saying William Bernhardt Greene had earned a doctorate degree in English. Dr. Willie, I thought. No one would have believed him if he'd of told us, but he never said a word. I miss those long talks when he would tell me about the Transcendentalists. They were sort of the first hippies, back in the eighteen hundreds.

Last night I finally finished the book I was reading the day of the boat wreck. I found a signed hardback copy of it in the box Willie's mom gave me, and decided finishing the book would be a way he'd want me to remember him.

I keep looking back at what happened on the island and what his death means. But I can't come up with an inspirational idea, something to say how he served a grand purpose or anything like that. For what it's worth, I know I'm better off knowing Willie. But don't ask me to explain how. An era of my life has passed, I think, and Willie would want me to figure it out. I know this much. It's like movement just at the edge of your vision. One of those times you get a creepy feeling of danger lurking behind you in the bushes, but nothing happens when you turn and look square on into the silent darkness, no matter how long you wait for your eyes to adjust.

The Trust Jesus Society

MORRISON JOPLIN HENDRIX JONES at first hated the name kids taunted him with as a child. But by age twenty he had accepted the inescapable name Mojo and a destiny that surely would follow.

Mojo's mother Betty Elizabeth Jones, named for both of her grandmothers, read to Mojo from birth. When he learned to read at five, she began to shove books in front of him each day—mostly biographies of people she thought were the world's great leaders. She told him he was born with a destiny. He soon believed her vision of his providence, and by the time he started school, he woke up every morning thinking about doing something the world would remember. Lead a movement for world peace. Cure cancer. End poverty. Maybe even win the Kentucky Derby or the World Series. He didn't discriminate among opportunities for fame, glory, or contributions to the betterment of mankind.

From the year Mojo turned ten he kept a reading list. He read books about the people his mom said were famous and important—Lincoln, Gandhi, Susan B. Anthony, Buddha, Catherine the Great, Emily Dickinson, Evil Knievel—though the language exceeded his reading level and spoke of places he had a hard time imagining. Mojo wrote each famous name in a journal and beside the name listed that person's message to the world. Lincoln—all men are created equal. Susan B. Anthony—women are equal to men. Evil Knievel—people cheer for you if you might die. And so on.

When his mother returned home pregnant in 1969 from Woodstock, the future of the child growing in her belly had not crossed her mind. There was not yet a grand vision for Mojo. She was in love. And the woven grass bracelet on her wrist provided all the evidence she needed that her circle of love was real.

Betty Betty, as Mojo's mother now insisted she be called, hitched her way home wearing a tie-dyed cotton dress, her only possessions a pair of leather sandals and a backpack holding a couple of paperbacks, a toothbrush, and a twenty-nine cent horoscope she'd lifted from the rack beside a grocery store checkout. She arrived on Labor Day to the Appalachian foothills in North Alabama, just a few miles from Fort Payne, and walked down a worn-out gravel road to tell her mother she was having a baby.

When Betty Betty arrived back home her dress was so dirty and threadbare from months of wear, plus four days of a rock concert in a muddy field and several days on the road that her mother Mary, an otherwise frugal woman who wasted nothing, simply threw away what was basically a thin rag not even suitable for washing the car.

The father never showed up. And the grass bracelet on Betty Betty's wrist soon fell apart. Her last contact with Mojo's father, whose birth name she later realized she'd never known, consisted of a single postcard postmarked from Oregon saying the man she loved was following the Grateful Dead on tour and hoping one day to find her again, because that would be true fate and cosmic karma, and proof that they were meant to be together. There was no return address on the postcard. It was signed

Yogi Bear, the name everyone called him, with a little peace sign drawn beneath the signature.

****

MOJO'S GRANDPARENTS BOUGHT HIS MOTHER A USED TWO-BEDROOM TRAILER and placed it on cement blocks on the side of their backyard, a tin skirt covering the wheels. Betty Betty went to work at the Piggly Wiggly as a cashier before Mojo was born, working right up to the last day before she gave birth the old-fashioned way. In a hospital. By the sixth month of her pregnancy, she quit talking of a natural birth in a yurt built by Mojo's father near a stream, surrounded by cantaloupe on the vine and flowerbeds bursting with forget-me-not and Sweet William.

****

MOJO SPENT LONG HOURS WITH THE TELEVISION AS HIS BABY-SITTER, grew up as the last kid chosen on the kickball team, and later the last kid chosen on the softball team.

He sat on the couch in the evenings as his mom pulled her feet up under her and asked him about his day while she massaged away the knots from standing at a cash register for six hours. "I'm going to teach you the Hare Krishna," Betty Betty would say. "And all about meditation to calm your soul when things get bad. We used to sit in a circle and meditate when I lived that summer in New York."

Betty Betty closed her eyes and turned her palms face up as her hands rested on her knees. Exhaling her breath slowly she said, "Do your fingers in a circle, like this." The musky scent of sandalwood permeated everything in the room, from the curtains to the sofa.

On Sundays, Mojo and Betty Betty attended the Free Will Baptist Church of Jesus Christ of Nazareth with Grandmother Mary and Papa Will, as he came to call his grandfather. The church was nestled in a strip of land between two ridges at the end of the alternately muddy and dusty road—depending on the latest heat spell or rainy weather—winding past their trailer. Papa Will was a deacon and passed the collection plate. Grandmother Mary sang in the choir with an incredibly high-pitched falsetto voice that Mojo assumed was how old women were supposed to sing. None of the congregation held their fingers in a circle, unless they were about to thump some kid behind an ear.

One bright June Sunday morning when he was eleven, Mojo felt God's call and walked down the aisle to join the church during the third verse of "Amazing Grace." The choir softly hummed the song as the preacher implored, "Don't you feel Jesus in your heart? How can you say no to the man whose precious blood ran into the ground at Calvary? Trust Jesus and walk on down here today to confess your sins." At the end of the church service, Mojo stood at the front of the church with a lump in his throat and tears on his cheeks as men in short-sleeve white shirts and wide paisley ties and women with full bosoms under long home-made flowing dresses filed by to give him a tight hug. The boys his age gave him a quick, limp handshake without looking him in the eye. Small red rambling roses, their branches tangled over the chain link fence around the church cemetery, sweetened the dry air blowing through the open windows.

He was baptized two weeks later in a nearby creek, along with two of his friends whose parents had nudged them into walking down the aisle after Mojo had gone first.

Betty Betty's interest in teaching him "the world's great religions, like Hindu and Yoga," had already begun to fade.

In high school he avoided PE by trying to learn the drums and playing in the high school band, though he never made it onto the football field at half-time. Despite his insistence for several years that teachers call him Morrison, or at least Morris, the kids called him Mojo and eventually he began to accept the name. When Mojo discovered songs that declared mojo a cool thing, he realized the name was part of his destiny. Even the Beatles, whose albums Betty Betty insisted he listen to, sang about mojo. Jim Morrison became his hero for having declared himself Mr. Mojo Risin' in "L.A. Woman." Of course, being a dead hero made him even more revered.

****

AFTER HIGH SCHOOL, MOJO SIGNED UP FOR CLASSES at the junior college. Grandmother Mary said she would pay as long as he made good grades. He cut weeds that filled the breeze with the smell of onions along the right-of-way for the electric co-op and saved his money. When he graduated two years later with his AA degree, he took a job in Birmingham as a salesman with his cousin's print shop. There, in the city, he discovered that a mojo was also a bag of magic charm, and a symbol of manhood. The name, once his burden, became his badge of honor. In all, Mojo managed to discover and purchase more than a dozen songs with the word *mojo* in them. "Got My Mojo Working," he would hum. He was a young man, everything before him and nothing to stop him, he told himself. Life was good. And sitting in his top drawer beside his bed, he kept the list he'd started so long ago, the list of how great people became great through a message the world needed to hear.

****

FOR THE THIRD TIME IN THE PAST TWO WEEKS, THE SAME GIRL WAS HAVING TOAST AND COFFEE, sitting on one of the stools at the counter. He saw her in the diner every morning, but this time she was right next to the stool at the end where Mojo always sat.

"Hello Mojo," Celestine said from behind the cash register. She had deep red bangs, almost purple, and a creme brulee complexion. She smiled, and he saw light reflect on the gold in both of her front teeth. A chorus of "Hello Mojo" echoed behind her as three waitresses and two cooks repeated her greeting. The trademark greeting for everyone through the front door was the main reason Mojo returned each day for coffee and scrambled eggs. The air was thick with odors of Murphy Oil soap, sizzling bacon and almost-burned toast.

Mojo eased onto his stool as a short, chubby waitress named Gladiola, the only white employee in the place, slid a cup of steaming coffee in front of him without asking what he wanted. He caught the girl's eye on the stool beside him.

"Morning."

"Hi," she said, quickly turning away with her head down. She put both hands around her coffee cup and said nothing more.

Mojo sipped his black coffee, sitting back so he could watch the woman a little. After a minute, he leaned forward on his elbows. "I saw you in here before."

She spun on her stool toward Mojo and smiled, obviously pleased that he had noticed her. She held out her hand. "I'm Martha."

****

MOJO'S THIRD DATE WITH MARTHA CONSISTED OF TWO GIANT SLICES OF PEPPERONI PIZZA at an outdoor cafe on Southside and a walk around the fountain at Five Points South to watch the skateboarders.

"Do you go to church?" Martha asked.

The next morning Mojo and Martha sat on the end of a pew near the middle of the Southside Bible Believers' Church. The church was what they called independent. No Baptist Convention or United Methodist pecking order to siphon off half the cash that flowed into the collection plate. No money sent on obscure missions to deliver translated King James bibles to starving children in places like Zantabia or Perutonia or some other place Mojo couldn't pronounce or find on a map. He saw plenty of poverty right where he lived, so he never understood that part about the church sending people to other places where God called. Mojo recognized a couple of the hymns and felt right at home joining in with the singing, though other than when he had returned home for Easter weekend to visit Betty Betty, he had not attended church in over a year. He was surprised when the preacher kept speaking past noon, with no hint of closing. Growing up, Mojo noticed that at twelve o'clock, a deacon or two would cough if the preacher seemed to still have a head of steam, and like magic the sermon would end a minute or two later.

But today the preacher kept up his rising and falling tones right through noon, and nearly half past the hour, he called on the choir to softly hum "Just As I Am" while he invited anyone who wanted Jesus to walk the aisle. When the preacher said to Trust Jesus, Mojo felt deja vu.

Walking into the bright light after the service Mojo felt

good. He'd missed church singing since moving to Birmingham, and this church had lots of hymns sprinkled through the service. He grabbed Martha's hand and felt her stiffen a little before she looked at him and relaxed. This date was the first time he'd held her hand in public, and she seemed uncertain about her friends seeing this intimacy at church.

Three weeks later, Mojo joined the church officially, and he and Martha went to Shoney's for the Sunday buffet to celebrate. Back in her apartment they sat on the couch and watched a Saints football game, not saying much. Mojo had called Betty Betty to tell her he had joined the congregation of his new girlfriend, but she only wanted to talk about herself so he said nothing. His mother seemed absorbed in getting ready for an afternoon on the river with a man she had met while she checked his groceries the day before.

Mojo could tell Martha was thinking hard about something. "What's on your mind?" he asked. He'd already learned her body language, and the way she leaned her head on his shoulder and looked down meant she had something to say.

"One of the guys at church wanted me to ask you something."

"Yeah?"

"There's this group at church, younger people. The elders don't even know about it."

Mojo laughed. "Sounds like a conspiracy."

"I'm serious," she said, slapping Mojo's leg. "This group is trying to do their own mission work. They think you might be a good person to join them. It's mostly guys, but some of us girls go to their meetings too. They call it The Trust Jesus Society."

Mojo sat up. The phrase Trust Jesus echoed through in his

head like a radio song you couldn't quit repeating. In that instant, he knew he would join this group, and that he would be changed, the way men he observed coming home from military service were changed, somehow more somber, serious, as if their childhood were a dream and they'd been born fully grown.

****

MARTHA'S BARELY AUDIBLE SNORING reminded Mojo of the whistle of the toy train he'd kept under his bed as a child. The precious train his grandfather had put together and tacked to thin plywood, so Mojo could slide the oval track under his bed, leaving the little red train station, tiny trees and miniature crossing gates in place. He'd spent hours alone with his train circling the board, puffing little oily smoke from its stack. Mojo leaned on one elbow and compared the freckled skin across the top of her chest with the white smooth skin on her breasts. Although they'd been together for months, sex with Martha still excited him as much as it had that first day. He never tired staring at her skin up close as she slept, close enough to see each pore. Close enough to smell the lingering flowery soap from her morning shower. He lay still without moving for half an hour, not wanting to wake her. Finally, Martha took a deep breath and rolled onto her back, her eyes opening.

Mojo smiled as she looked up at him.

"How long have you been watching me?" Martha asked, just above a whisper.

"Not long. You were so peaceful."

Martha smiled, revealing a row of straight white teeth. She sat up suddenly and reached for her watch on the bedside table. Her smile vanished. "Oh Gosh, I'm late. Why didn't you wake me?" She threw off the covers and bent over, gathering her white cotton panties and bra, navy skirt and white blouse as she rushed to the bathroom.

"Looked like you needed to rest," Mojo said to Martha's back as she walked into the bathroom, leaving the door open. "Thought just this once a long lunch hour wouldn't be such a big deal."

He watched Martha look at herself in the mirror. Her lipstick had faded to hints of color on the edges of her lips, leaving her face pale. He saw her blush and imagined she was thinking of what they had just done.

Mojo believed her when Martha told him she'd never done things like this before. But he knew she had read thousands of books and she had to wonder about the many sexual acts she had not tried. Martha had told Mojo that her only other lover, during her senior year of college, had been as shy as she, insisting on turning out the lights before a rush of groping and grunting in the dark. Martha said the affair had lasted two months until graduation, but never got past him climbing on top of her for a couple of minutes for a hurried burst of passion, then rolling over and sleeping. Mojo knew she liked the way he made her feel loved.

"Can you drop me by the library?" Martha asked as she stroked her hair with a brush from her purse. She turned her head from side to side to see if she had hidden the effects of her lunch hour passion.

"Sure," Mojo said, laughing a little. "Do I have to let you off a block away again like I'm your old Dad and you don't want the other kids to see me?"

****

MOJO PULLED THE VOLKSWAGON to the curb behind a white delivery truck that was blocking half the lane, parked with the sliding door open. He caught a faint smell of fruit, maybe cantaloupe. Two men unloaded boxes of lemons and lettuce through the side door of the Downtown Café. Martha leaned over and kissed his cheek quickly before stepping to the sidewalk. She hurried around the corner to walk the last block to the library, her shirt sleeves blowing in the light breeze. He watched her disappear and thought of the glow in her cheeks. He wondered if others would notice the difference in her normally pale face.

Mojo backed up a few feet and steered left around the delivery truck into the busy downtown traffic. He aimed his car down the wide Twentieth Street toward the heart of Southside's Five Points area, where he would spend the afternoon calling on small businesses, restaurants, law offices and retail shops selling the services of his printing company. He thought of the business as his company, though in truth his cousin and her husband owned it. Mojo had been promised an opportunity to buy into maybe ten percent one day, and he had taken their offer as a goal. No one would outwork or out hustle him.

He had to hurry. He had lots to do before five thirty, when he planned to meet Jason, the partner he'd been assigned in the Trust Jesus Society when he joined months earlier. Mojo had purchased a case of blue spray paint that morning. He smiled, thinking of his mission.

****

FEW PEOPLE EVER FOUND GOD'S APPOINTED MISSION IN LIFE, Mojo repeated over and over as he drove south on Interstate 65, finally quoting the phrase out loud to Jason who had missed the breakfast meeting that day. These were the first words Mojo heard that morning from the young leader of the

Bible study group that Martha had encouraged him to join nearly six months earlier, though mostly they talked about what high-
ways had not yet been hit by their spray paint teams. The group
was by invitation only, and all men in the meetings except for
Martha and two other girlfriends. Jason sat reading a state highway map and tracing roads with his finger.

"How long you been in the group?" Mojo asked.

"Year or so I guess," Jason said. "At first I thought it was just
younger people in the church meeting on Wednesday morning
for bacon and eggs and Bible study."

"Was Nate the one who started it?"

"Yeah I guess," Jason said, shrugging.

The leader of the group, Nathaniel Castille, seemed to be
loved by everyone in the church. While he held no official position, Mojo noticed that on Sundays everyone spoke to the dark-
haired young man with the friendly smile and eyes that flashed
like diamonds, and he always called them by name. First name if
they were younger than he, and a polite Mr. or Mrs. if older.

"I like Nate," Mojo said, thinking how Nate would come up
to Mojo every Sunday to shake his hand like a best friend. And
the way he would introduce Mojo to church members as "my
friend Morrison, but we just call him Mojo."

****

MOJO NEARED AN OVERPASS and saw the tall, neatly
spray painted letters: *Trust Jesus.* He smiled, knowing someone in
his group had been this way before. His assignment today—one
of nearly a dozen he'd taken with Jason—was to drive one hour
south and check each paint job, repainting any that were faded
or had been covered over by state road crews.

Mojo soon passed the point he'd planned to turn around,

somewhere near Clanton. He'd not stopped once, as each sign was intact and easily read. He was almost disappointed that no one had tampered with his group's work. So he kept driving, and Jason kept talking, as he had almost from the start of the drive.

"So what do you think, Mojo? You up for it?" Jason finally asked, as he folded the map. Mojo knew he was talking about a true mission trip, a drive west into territory not ever touched by the Trust Jesus Society.

Mojo nodded. The plan excited him. And though he never said a word, he felt that the destiny his mother had drilled into him might be tied to this mission idea. He didn't know what Martha would think. In recent weeks, she had found an excuse to be together every night.

Last weekend when she'd asked if he thought they would get married, he knew that something had to change in his relationship, one way or the other. He had been thrilled when she gave him his own key to her apartment. But he didn't want to give up yet on doing something important before he settled down.

"Let's do it," Mojo finally answered Jason. "I bet we could cover 300 miles a day. If we left on a Saturday and went right through for three weeks in a big circle, we could get to the edge of the Northwest and back I bet. No one in our group has ever taken on a mission this big."

****

MARTHA PUT HER HEAD IN MOJO'S LAP as she lay back on the couch with her feet propped on the arm. The news blared on television, but neither paid much attention to the program. Mojo was telling Martha of his dream, of igniting interest nationwide of the mysterious appearance of Trust Jesus on every highway in the country. Martha was quiet. Mojo asked her if she felt all right, but she said she was fine. From her forced smile he could tell something wasn't exactly right.

"I'm not a nut or even a religious fanatic," Mojo said, his voice soft as if he were really talking to himself. "But this country needs something to pull the people together, something to rally behind as we face more drugs, more murders. And the world hates us."

Martha looked away. "I don't think you should go."

Mojo held Martha's head up and stood up. They'd not yet had a single word of disagreement. He simply shook his head. "This is important. It would only be three weeks. I've already worked it out with my job."

"I just don't think it's right to be off like that for so long."

"Martha, I don't get it. You're the one who got me in this group. What could possibly be wrong with me going on a mission trip like this?"

Martha said nothing, looking out the window.

Mojo leaned toward her and tried to put his arm around her, but she pushed him away.

"Martha, I'm sorry. What's wrong?"

Her face showed little emotion.

"I don't have to go if it upsets you."

He forced his arm around her. She didn't push him away this time; he held her like that with her head against his chest, thinking how much he didn't understand women.

"It's Nate," Martha said, after several minutes.

"What about Nate?"

"He came over here while you were gone on the mission last Saturday."

"What did he want? You didn't tell me he came over."

Mojo watched Martha lower her eyes. He realized Nate had not been there on God's work. "Did something happen?"

Mojo could see Martha thinking, hesitant. "He tried to kiss me."

****

MOJO POUNDED ON THE APARTMENT DOOR waiting for Nate to turn the lock from inside. Nothing. He knocked with his knuckles as hard as he could stand, then hammered the door with his fists until an older man down the hall opened his door a crack and peeked out at Mojo.

Mojo stared at the man, then turned and stomped down the stairs, not wanting to wait for the elevator or the police if the old guy decided to call them. Mojo slammed the stairwell door and hurried out the apartment building front entrance into the bright light of a cloudless day.

For a moment Mojo stopped and thought, wondering where to go next to find Nate. His hands shook, unaccustomed to the fire pulsing through his veins. He was looking down the sidewalk, deciding which way to go, when Nate turned the corner on foot and walked his direction. A huge smile spread across Nate's face as he recognized Mojo from half a block away. Mojo started toward Nate, fists tight against his sides, his chin jutting forward. He said nothing as he slammed his fist into Nate's stomach. Nate fell to his knees, then forward onto the pavement. He rolled onto his side gasping. Two men and a woman walking nearby stopped, but no one came closer than ten feet. Mojo bent down and poked his finger into Nate's face. "If you ever come near Martha again you will meet God sooner than you think." Mojo rose and turned toward the three pedestrians, who moved aside as he walked quickly down the sidewalk. His hands were shaking. He'd never hit someone, and didn't know where that side of him had been hiding his whole life.

The sun steamed through Mojo's shirt, and his back began sticking to the cloth. He walked several blocks with no destination in mind and suddenly realized he didn't know exactly where he was. The sidewalk glittered with broken beer bottles. He stopped to decide on a new direction and kicked at a weed growing through the concrete.

As he walked, the sun dropped behind the downtown buildings and eventually streetlights crackled and buzzed as they came on one by one. It had been dark for an hour when Mojo bounded up the front steps of Martha's apartment building. Although he had his key to her door, he knocked and waited for her to let him in.

She was freshly showered with makeup on, as if going out, but Mojo knew she never left the apartment this late. She offered him tea, and he waited on the couch as she poured the sweet tea over ice and placed the glass on a round stone coaster on the glass-top coffee table in front of him.

"I'm sorry," Martha said. "I didn't mean to upset you. I probably made too much of a little thing. I don't think Nate meant anything. Let's just forget about it."

Mojo took a drink and was thinking of why she would say it was nothing now that he'd slugged Nate. He didn't want to yell at Martha, but something inside him was yelling. He forced his voice under control and spoke slowly: "What do you mean he didn't mean anything? Did he try to kiss you or not?"

"Well, it seemed like he did. But maybe it was just friendly."

Mojo stood up and placed the glass gently on the table. He walked to the window and stared out. Minutes passed and neither spoke. He finally turned to look at Martha and lowered his voice just above a whisper. He hands were shaking. "I'll be back in three weeks, after my mission trip." He turned and walked out the front door before Martha could respond. He heard his name behind him as the door closed.

****

MOJO PULLED INTO THE BP STATION JUST OVER THE CALIFORNIA STATE LINE and stepped out of the car to stretch. He placed the gas nozzle into the tank and stood looking around as the tank filled. One week. He never thought he'd make the California turn this fast, but leaving Jason behind had helped. He like traveling at his own pace. His decision to only hit every third or fourth overpass was the key. He was feeling good. About himself and his future.

He'd made some decisions as he spent the hours unaccompanied on the highway. He knew he wanted to marry Martha and would ask her when he returned. Then they would find another church, maybe move outside town where they could have a small plot of land. Raise kids one day. Things were clear to him now. The time alone was all he needed. And when everything was set with Martha, he would write about the trip. Go on talk shows. Find a way to say something important and get on with his life. The woman pumping gas across from him smiled, and Mojo realized he'd been smiling. He thought he should call Martha again and tell her he was on his way home, but the call two days ago had only made things more strained. He'd wait until he could talk in person. He could fix it in person.

Mojo laid the map on the trunk and followed the interstates with his finger. It took him only a few seconds to decide the route home. He'd circle through the state for one day and drop down to Interstate 20 for the return trip. He focused on the future. With Martha at his side, he'd take his message north and south, east and west using television and radio. And there would be a book, not just articles, but a real book. National TV would want to know who was behind the Trust Jesus movement. And he would take over the story. Own it. Make it his story. The movement was not his idea originally, but he was making the movement his now. He knew that any day some reporter would take note of the signs popping up across the country. And the world would sit up and watch the story unfold.

Mojo signaled with the blinker that he was merging into the heavy traffic. He pressed the accelerator and found room between two eighteen wheelers.

****

THE SIGN AT THE STATE LINE SAID "WELCOME TO ALABAMA THE BEAUTIFUL," and the message seemed fitting to Mojo. He found himself speeding up as he neared home after making the return trip in a week. The open windows whistled and drowned Mojo's voice as he sang along with one song after another. The trip had taken only two weeks instead of the three Jason had planned. Mojo had driven and painted well into the night almost every night, sleeping five or six hours and stopping only for gas and sandwiches.

Mojo had watched through his rearview mirror earlier as the sun dropped below the horizon outside Jackson, Mississippi. He figured he could make Martha's house by ten or so and catch her right before bedtime. He had a lot to tell her.

He found a parking spot only half a block away. Reaching over the seat, Mojo grabbed the small gift bag that held the silver and jade handmade necklace he'd purchased at a roadside gas station that doubled as a jewelry outlet for a nearby tribe in Arizona. He opened his door and stepped onto the sidewalk, felt the stored summer heat in the concrete even though it was long past sundown.

When he reached Martha's apartment he opted for the stairs, knowing the slow elevators here didn't suit his feelings tonight.

At Martha's door Mojo slid the key soundlessly into the lock. He heard giggling at the same time he pushed the door open. As the door swung back, Mojo saw Martha sitting cross-legged on the couch against the opposite wall, pushing Nate's hand away as he tried to feed her ice cream with a spoon. He saw that both had chocolate smeared around their mouths and running down their chins. They looked at Mojo, their eyes wide. Neither of them was wearing anything. No one spoke.

****

MOJO PILED FURNITURE, CLOTHES AND EVEN HIS ONE RUG INTO A LARGE PILE behind his apartment. He wadded newspaper and stuffed it into openings in the pile and held a match under the edges in several spots. Soon flames began to chase the spinning smoke, and it grew to a raging fire.

Mojo reached down and picked up a cardboard box. Inside were the biographies his mother had encouraged him to study of famous people he had admired. One by one he removed biographies of Lincoln, Washington, Robert E. Lee, tossing them through the dumpster opening, and finally lobbed the remaining books at once over onto the plastic bags of garbage that filled the metal bin nearly to the top.

He took one last look at his notebook, dog-eared and filled with his notes of why certain people were great and important. He spun the book into the center of the flames.

Mojo walked back inside his empty apartment and counted out the rent for the month, placing a stack of twenty dollar bills into an envelope. He dialed his landlord and left a message that he was moving out and the current month's rent was on the kitchen counter. Then he telephoned his mother, leaving a message after the machine came on that he was moving west and would call when he got there. He hung up the phone, then ripped it from the wall and placed it on the counter beside the envelope. He locked the door behind him and dropped the key through the mail slot.

Mojo moved a case of spray paint from the trunk of his car into the front seat. The tart smell of burning plastic stung the inside of his nostrils. He slid a homemade DVD of Jim Morrison into the player and turned up the sound. All fifteen recordings on the DVD were the same song: "L.A. Woman." Mr. Mojo Risin'. Mr. Mojo Risin'. Mr. Mojo Risin'.

Into the night he drove, stopping at overpass after overpass. Truly, he was a man with a mission. His message clear. His place in history crystallizing with each stop. By morning, Mojo's fingers were blue, and his steering wheel was blue and tacky from the spray paint.

The sun rose behind him as he pushed the car past 70, past 80, on to 100. He could feel the energy surging through the floor from the hum of rubber on pavement, vibrating up the soles of his feet, making his heart dance. Behind him and far into his future were signs, signs from God with a life-changing message. When he closed his eyes he could see them.

Trust ~~Jesus~~ No One

Trust ~~Jesus~~ No One

Trust ~~Jesus~~ No One

The Downtown Club

Amanda pulled a silky black stocking over her foot. The rays of the summer sunset washed the bedroom wall behind her in red-orange, exaggerating the curve of her leg in its shadow. She sat upright in the straight-back chair as she smoothed the material over her freshly shaved skin. She caught her image in the mirror behind the door and considered why men always grew excited by stockings and garters. With a foot resting on the chair seat, Amanda ran one hand up her leg along the side of her thigh to the black lace panties. She turned to see the deep cleavage created by her push-up bra. Outlines of her small breasts were visible through the lace.

She'd worn the garter and stockings, along with the high-cut panties and matching bra, only once, three years earlier. She half-smiled, briefly, remembering the incredible sex she had enjoyed with her husband after that Halloween party. Three months later, he was dead. She'd found him face down on the jogging path near their home when he failed to return from his morning run. The doctor said he'd carried the heart defect his entire life and there was nothing anyone could have done.

Amanda squeezed into a short black leather skirt and slid her arms into a tight red silk blouse with a deep V in front. The skirt covered the black underwear, though the dark stocking tops showed when she sat with her legs crossed. A pair of four-inch heels covered in black satin completed the outfit.

From its box inside a shopping bag, Amanda lifted an expen-sive blond wig with short curls, purchased that afternoon. She repositioned the wig a couple of times and was satisfied the hair looked natural. She applied heavy charcoal eye shadow over her eyelids, accenting the corner of her eyes with a bit of silver.

Standing in front of the mirror, Amanda posed to see if she could look comfortable in the outfit. Not bad for forty-five. She sprayed perfume she'd taken from her daughter's dressing table heavily behind each ear and picked up the large purse. She was ready. As she walked out of the bedroom, she thought about her husband's pistol under the mattress, but she knew she couldn't use a gun for this.

****

Amanda sat in her car with the air conditioner blowing into her face to fend off the muggy Mississippi heat. It was still eighty-eight an hour after sundown. She'd backed into a space on the side of the cinder block building that housed the Downtown Club, wedged between two huge metal buildings with faded logos painted one on top of the other until none were legible. She thought about how her comfortable life had changed over the past months, at last leading her to this tired part of Jackson she'd never seen or even knew existed. She noticed the row of shotgun houses across the street, plywood nailed over each window and scattered weeds standing two feet tall in a tiny front yard that had once held grass where children must have laughed and played.

She looked down at the smooth stockings covering her legs and knew she could easily find a man tonight. Not that she had much interest in sex. That could wait. Like everything else she'd put on hold for the past year. Her world had shrunk to a tiny two-bedroom house since she brought her daughter Pam home from the hospital to recover from being beaten to near death.

Amanda's friends didn't understand, and most had drifted away as she refused to go out with them on weekends. No one knew of the hours she'd spent sitting in her car watching the man who'd attacked her daughter as he'd come and go from his various hangouts.

She checked the wig again in the car mirror. The curls made Amanda think of Pam, who'd left a bad marriage only to end up half bloody and unconscious for hours in an alley after being picked up in a bar. And how Pam refused to leave the house after dark now.

Amanda leaned toward the mirror and dabbed a tissue on the tears that had formed in her eyes. She went through a check-list of the items she'd placed in the purse: a small pill, a wrapped package of cocaine and a new pair of poultry shears. She reached for the cell phone to call her mother and check on Pam, but decided it best not to call now. She turned off the phone and dropped it into her purse.

****

Amanda stood in the front doorway of the Downtown Club for a few seconds as her eyes adjusted to the dark room. The bar was hazy with smoke from cigars and cigarettes. A dozen or so men stood around the pool tables in back, and a row of men slouched on the bar stools on the right. A few wore dark work shirts with their names sewn over the pocket; others wore jeans and tee shirts, with tattoos of flags, motorcycles or curvy women peeking under the sleeves. She saw only two women, seated close to a man in a corner booth. Most of the men were there for a quick beer on their way home from the welding shops, parts stores and used car lots that surrounded the bar.

Above the bar mirror, bumper stickers papered the wall, some of the old white ones now brown. Ski Mississippi. American by Birth, Southern by the Grace of God. Wallace for President. Gun Control Means Using Both Hands. Problem with My Driving? Call 1-800-EAT-SHIT. Work Is For People Who Can't Fish.

The man she knew as Larsen sat alone at a table past the end of the bar near three pool tables, wearing a starched cowboy shirt with pearl snaps and pressed jeans. For the first time Amanda realized he was handsome, chiseled chin, high cheek bones and a close shave. She wondered why his looks hadn't registered with her before.

As Amanda walked slowly behind the long row of bar stools, the room grew quieter. She found a stool near the end of the bar, not far from Larsen's table. The bartender flipped a small white towel over his shoulder that he'd been using to wipe freshly washed mugs.

"Yes ma'am?" he said, lifting his eyebrows as if asking an obvious question.

"Vodka. Rocks. Double," Amanda said, loud enough for Larsen to hear. Opening her purse, she removed a pack of Virginia Slims and a twenty-dollar bill. She placed the twenty on the bar and shook a cigarette from the pack. The bartender reached into his shirt pocket for matches, lit one and held the flame a few inches in front of her. She leaned toward the match, allowing the bartender a look inside her blouse at the black lace pushing her breasts together. She remained expressionless when he realized he'd been caught looking, as if his glance down her blouse was expected and appreciated but wasn't to be acknowledged. The bartender deposited the drink in front of her on a thin napkin.

Amanda could see herself in the mirror above the bar, behind bottles of Jim Beam and Jack Daniels Bourbon, Taaka Vodka, Gilbey's Gin, and a pyramid of cheap glasses stacked upside down. She looked in the mirror and pretended to find something wrong with the makeup around her eyes. She turned toward the bartender as she stood up and clutched her purse. "Where's your ladies room, Sugar?"

"Back in that corner, behind the pool tables."

Amanda picked up her drink and walked toward the restroom, taking a route that allowed her to walk close enough to Larsen for him to smell the trail of perfume. In the restroom she leaned toward the smudged mirror as she twirled her lipstick open. She slid the tip once between her lips from left to right, coating both with the thick red color. She checked her wig, then gulped the vodka and swished the liquor around in her mouth to make sure she had the smell on her breath. She spit the mouthful of vodka into the nasty sink and poured out the rest while holding her fingers over the ice. Looking up and seeing the curly wig, she wondered if Pam had stood before this same mirror that night. Amanda reached up to touch her face, suddenly seeing Pam's face in the mirror and the deep red scar from the knife Larsen had turned on Pam after ripping the blade from her hand as she tried to fight him off.

Amanda refilled the drink with tap water and walked back to her bar stool. For the next ten minutes she sipped the water to regain control, before downing the last few drops. She wouldn't cry again. She slid the glass across the bar and caught the bartender's attention. "Another, please."

The bartender dumped her glass into the sink, picked up a fresh tumbler and filled it with ice and a double vodka. He put the glass on a square napkin in front of her. He picked up a five-dollar bill from the ten and five still laying on the bar.

Amanda slowly sipped the vodka, thinking that a couple of swallows might even help relax her. Soon the only way out would be to finish what she started. In the mirror behind the bar she checked to see if Larsen was watching. He was. She put her elbows on the bar and crossed her legs, allowing the tight skirt to slide up her thigh, showing the top of the stockings. After a moment, she rocked sideways on the stool and pulled the skirt lower. Larsen was practically staring now, but didn't realize she was watching him in the mirror. She could tell he didn't recognize her. The charges against Larsen were dropped when Amanda wouldn't let Pam testify, and the months of fitful sleep and second-guessing that followed for Amanda made her lose twenty-five pounds. A change of hair color and length completed the disguise, especially with enough leg showing to keep Larsen's eyes focused away from her face.

The bartender served a couple of beers at the other end of the bar, then wandered back to stand in front of Amanda. She spoke first. "What kind of stuff you got on the jukebox?"

"Oh, you know, the usual. It's a pretty good selection. Dwight Yoakam, Brad Paisley, Vince Gill, Garth Brooks, Faith Hill, Confederate Railroad. Some older stuff, too. George Jones, David Allen Coe, Willie Nelson. Here, I'm buying if you're flying." The bartender grabbed two dollars from the tip jar and held the bills toward her. She reached for the money, knowing the cash was just to see her bend over the jukebox.

She smiled as she took the money. "Anything you want to hear?"

"Whatever you like is fine, Sweetheart."

She sipped her drink as she walked to the jukebox swaying her hips. As she bent over to punch the letters and numbers, she knew every man nearby was watching her and hoping the skirt would ride higher up the backs of her thighs.

Johnny Cash launched into the second verse of "Ring of Fire" as Amanda started back to the bar. She stopped off briefly at the ladies room, where she again replaced the vodka with water. She walked past Larsen and sat sideways on the bar stool, giving him a quick view between her legs when she swung around to face the bar. From Larsen's viewpoint an inch of thigh above the stocking tops would be visible.

Amanda drank her water for another fifteen minutes. Occasionally she spoke to the bartender, who always returned to her end of the bar after he served the other customers.

As she finished the second double water, the bartender slid a drink in front of her. "Compliments of the gentleman over there." He tilted his head toward Larsen.

Amanda felt her pulse throbbing at her throat. It was happening just as Pam had described it. She took a deep breath and turned back to the bartender. "I don't usually take drinks from strangers," she said, attempting to sound a bit drunk.

"Hey, it's up to you," he said and stepped back, standing a few steps farther away than before and letting the conversation go cold.

Obviously, Larsen wasn't someone the bartender wanted to compete with. She wondered if Larsen still carried the same nickel-finish pistol he'd forced between Pam's teeth.

Amanda let the glass sit on the bar for a minute, inhaled deeply once again to calm her heart, picked the drink up and turned in her seat. She held the glass up toward Larsen in a toast. Larsen picked up his can of beer and returned the gesture, leaning back in his chair with his legs crossed. His boots reflected red and blue neon beer signs.

Turning to face the bar, Amanda let the skirt slide up another inch to show a fraction of the garter. Enjoy it while you can, you smug bastard. I hope you remember this for the rest of your life.

For ten minutes she sipped her drink and watched Larsen in the mirror, not wanting to appear too eager. Whenever someone walked past Larsen, he was quick to speak and seemed to know everyone by first name. He had an ever-present smile and even the two women stopped to talk as they walked to the ladies room and laughed at something he said. He seemed very at ease with himself, and the regulars here obviously liked him. She found herself asking how he could've done what Pam said.

Amanda wondered if Larsen was used to waiting out new women he met. When the bartender returned from checking his customers at the far end of the bar, she asked him to take Larsen a beer. She stood up and walked right behind the bartender as he delivered the can to the table. Amanda saw the looks of disappointment from the four men nearby playing pool, who must have had thoughts about their own chances with the whore in the short leather skirt. "Mind if I join you? I hate to drink alone."

"Please do," Larsen said, halfway standing and reaching to help with her chair. He didn't appear surprised to see her, but was gracious like most men she knew in the South when meeting a woman the first time.

"I'm Casey. What's your name?"

"Everyone just calls me Larsen. I don't think I've seen you in here before."

"No, you ain't seen me here. I just moved into town. I split with my old man in Hattiesburg and moved up here to try something new. Everywhere I went down there I ran into one of his sisters or his drinking buddies." She tried not to pour on the country too much. She wanted to sound uneducated, not stupid.

"Well, you might like it here. Just about everyone that comes in this bar is a regular. We don't see many new people here. Especially any as good looking as you."

Larsen was smart. She knew he was venturing a safe compliment to see where it might lead. She smiled and didn't act offended.

It worked. He grew a little bolder. "Are you meeting someone here?"

"No. Just wanted to get out of that little apartment and have a drink around some people." Amanda fumbled in her purse, acting a bit drunk as she removed her cigarettes. She shook out the last Virginia Slim and held the cigarette in front of her face. She'd even thought to empty the pack of all but three cigarettes before leaving home. "Light?"

Larsen reached into his pocket and pulled out a worn Zippo lighter, brass showing at the corners where there had once been chrome. He flicked his thumb across the little wheel, lighting the wick on the first try. He reached over to hold the flame for her. Light from the florescent tubes above the pool tables caught the left side of his face and she saw the sparkle of a tiny diamond-stud earring. Pam's earring. She bit the inside of her cheek to keep from screaming. Just get through it, she told herself, breathing through her nose with her lips pressed together. She forced a smile. Then she leaned over to light the cigarette, giving Larsen a clear view of her breasts.

"Thank you, Sweetie." She took a long drag on the cigarette and tilted her head back as she blew the smoke. It tasted good. She was surprised she was ever able to quit.

Larsen said nothing, merely nodded as he slid the lighter back into his jeans pocket and crossed his legs. His own cigarette sat on the ashtray, burning. Smoke hovered over the table, slowly spiraling toward the ceiling. She noticed his boots were polished to a fine sheen, which fit with his pressed clothes and well-kept fingernails.

Leaning forward, Amanda gave Larsen her made-up personal history and then steered the conversation back to him as she stubbed out the cigarette. "So what's your story?" she asked.

"Not much to it," Larsen said. "I run liquor stores. Hang out here after work."

She tried not to stare at the earring by looking into Larsen's eyes. "There's got to be more than that. Did you grow up here?"

"I was raised up in the Delta before moving to Jackson twenty-five years ago."

She asked a few more questions, but he would say little. Even as Larsen kept up his conversation with Amanda, he paused every time someone walked past, calling each person by name. His personal questions to his friends about this one's daughter's soccer team or that one's new job surprised Amanda.

Amanda sipped the vodka drink, allowing the liquor to melt the ice and water itself down, and wondered if she somehow had Larsen's story wrong. She had to be sure. "I like your little diamond. What's the story behind that?" she asked.

He didn't answer, just watched her.

The muscles in his jaw tightened as he searched her eyes. In that moment she knew Pam's story was true. It was all true. She was careful to stay cool. Play dumb, she told herself. "You're not gay are you?" she asked, laughing like it was a joke.

Larsen cocked his head to the side and said nothing as he looked hard into her eyes, a half smile showing he thought she was a little funny.

She knew what she needed to know and tried again to break the tension before he said anything. She picked up her empty cigarette package, crumpled it and mumbled, "Oh, damn." She reached into her purse and pulled out four one-dollar bills. Smiling, she looked into Larsen's eyes. "Honey, do you mind getting me some smokes? Virginia Slim 100s?"

Larsen accepted the bills and walked toward the cigarette machine near the front door. As soon as his back was turned, Amanda reached into her purse and removed a small pill. She looked around. No one was watching closely. She moved her hand over Larsen's beer as if reaching for the ashtray and dropped the pill into his beer. She picked up her own drink and walked to the restroom, repeating the switch of water for vodka. She reached up and fluffed her hair a little, leaving it slightly imperfect. Opening her lipstick, she ran it across her lips, coloring both in a single stroke, not bothering to check it in the mirror.

Larsen was waiting at the table. She lit another cigarette, took a drag, then tilted her head back and downed the last swallow of water. Larsen immediately held his beer up to the bartender and motioned for another round. He then downed his beer and, she hoped, the pill. She had no experience with what her lifelong friend Benny called the Date Rape Pill. When Benny—the only friend who knew what she was doing—brought the tablet to her house, he told her to watch for signs that the drug was taking effect and then get Larsen out of the bar quickly—or she might not be able to get him out at all.

Amanda leaned back in her chair and again held up her drink toward Larsen. "Here's to new places and new friends. And to women who want to take back their lives." When Larsen's expression was slightly puzzled at her words, she simply smiled at him. And her smile was genuine.

She placed the watered-down drink to her lips and took a big swallow as she leaned back and crossed her legs. Larsen was taking a long drink of his beer, but she saw him look down. She shifted in her chair, so he could see above the stockings to her garters.

A pool table was open behind Larsen. She uncrossed her legs and momentarily held her knees three or four inches apart as she leaned forward, revealing the insides of her thighs all the way to the lacy panties. In a low, husky voice, she said, "Want to play pool?"

"Sure," Larsen said, smiling again for the first time since she'd asked about his earring.

She walked to the table, wobbling slightly. She could feel the three quarters she had stacked inside her left shoe in the ladies room. The quarters made her walk unbalanced. She'd seen the trick on a spy show on the History Channel.

Larsen put coins into the pool table and racked the balls. "You want to break?"

"Sure baby," she said, applying chalk to the cue stick.

Larsen walked behind her as she bent over to make the pool

shot. The cue ball made a crisp, loud crack as it sent the triangle of balls spinning around the table, though no balls went in.

"Good break. Bad luck," Larsen said, seeing how hard she'd hit the cue ball.

"Yeah, my old man used to take me to play a lot." The story was partially true, and she knew she could back up the statement with her play. She and her husband had played often a few years before when they'd bought a pool table for their den.

Neither she nor Larsen played well. She made a couple of easy shots to show she could, but she intentionally missed several shots to buy time and to flash Larsen until his interest peaked. She could tell he enjoyed watching her bend over and stretch to make shots. Everyone around could see plenty of leg and lots of cleavage when she leaned forward to study each shot. Finally Amanda sank the eight ball in an easy shot. To miss it would have been obvious. Larsen was beginning to appear drunk.

"I get bored real quick. Let's go have another drink." She tossed her cue stick on the pool table as she walked back to their chairs. Larsen followed.

For another twenty minutes she managed to carry on a conversation. She mostly asked Larsen questions about Jackson, places to eat, other clubs, all of which he answered with short sentences. She noticed he was having trouble concentrating. She was certain the pill was beginning to take effect.

It was now or never. She scooted her chair closer to Larsen and leaned into him, putting her hand on his knee and letting her fingers trail lightly down the inside of his leg. She knew he could smell her, despite the smoke and stale beer. "Do you like to dance? Is there somewhere we could go? I'm tired of this place."

"I don't like to dance." Larsen slurred his words now. "But we can go somewhere else if you want to."

"Then drink up," Amanda said. Larsen tipped back the full beer he'd just ordered. As he drained it, she slid two empty cans from the table into her purse, using a napkin so they would only have Larsen's fingerprints on them. She squeezed his thigh and stood up. "Let's go."

Larsen dropped several bills on the table, and the two of them walked outside. Just as it had when she walked in, the entire place grew momentarily quieter. She heard a hushed comment about Larsen getting lucky, followed by muffled laughter.

"Where's your car, honey?" Amanda asked. Larsen motioned toward his white El Dorado.

When they reached the car she spun around and leaned back against the driver's side door. She grabbed the front of Larsen's shirt and pulled him to her as she put her arms around his neck. In his eyes she could see a mixture of confusion and desire. The pill was slowing Larsen, but he managed to put one hand down to her skirt to feel her thigh through the leather. She rubbed her palm down the front of Larsen's pants across his zipper, knowing that he couldn't think straight once she had him aroused and drugged at the same time. She cupped his half-erect penis through his jeans, closing her eyes as she did and talking to herself. Just get through it. It's almost over. "Mmmmmmmmmmmmmmm, nice," she whispered in his ear.

She allowed him to move her skirt up, pushing his hand away once he briefly felt the silk panties. His other hand was around her neck, as he bent to kiss her roughly. She could smell the alcohol on his smoky breath and the acrid bar smoke that had saturated both their clothes. She turned her head after a second, pulled his head forward and put her mouth to his ear. "Not out here, Baby. Let's go somewhere private."

Larsen's hands were moving over her body, but she managed to step to the side. "Let's get in the car, Sugar."

After Larsen found his keys, she unlocked the doors. She had to help him into the driver's seat and went around to the passenger side. She dropped the keys onto the floor.

"Where're my keys?" Larsen asked. The sentence came out as one long word.

"It's all right Baby, let's just sit here." Amanda turned in the seat, so she could scan the parking lot over his shoulder. She reached over with her right hand and fondled him lightly. "Let me take care of you first. Just sit back and relax."

Larsen leaned back in the seat. His arms fell to his sides.

Amanda left her hand in his lap, rubbing the outside of Larsen's pants just enough to keep him occupied. When his eyes closed after a minute, she stopped. She caught a scream in her throat when Larsen grabbed a handful of her hair behind her head. She reacted without thinking and pulled away. The wig came off in Larsen's hand.

"Whatthehell…" he said, struggling to focus as he looked up at Amanda. His eyes grew wide. "Hey you bitch, don't I know you?"

Amanda lunged at Larsen and grabbed his head with both hands, slamming it into the steering wheel. He pounded his fist into her ribs, but she held onto his head and drove it into the steering wheel again and again. She finally realized the screaming was coming from her own throat. Larsen grew limp. She released his head, and it slumped to the side. Blood dripped from his nose, and his face was swollen and red.

Amanda looked around the parking lot at the cars. No one else was around. Larsen remained still. She shook him by the shoulder. No response.

After putting on latex gloves from her purse, Amanda began working as quickly as she could. She picked up the keys and wiped them with a scarf, then inserted the ignition key. She removed the large wrapped package of cocaine and threw it onto the floor on her side where it would be clearly visible from outside the car. Next she opened a smaller plastic bag of cocaine and placed it on the center console. She wiped a tiny mirror clean of prints. Taking Larsen's right hand, she pressed his thumb and fingers onto the glass. She put a teaspoon of the cocaine on the mirror, along with a short McDonald's straw she'd cut in half, and placed them all on the console next to the bag of drugs.

She pinched a small amount of the cocaine between her thumb and finger and forced it into Larsen's mouth. She was careful not to use too much, taking just a tiny bit to show cocaine in Larsen's blood if he was tested. She sprinkled cocaine powder onto Larsen's top lip and down the front of his shirt.

From her purse, she removed the two Bud Light beer cans. She turned both cans upside down and shook a few remaining drops onto Larsen's shirt where it mixed with drops of blood. She threw one can on the floor and placed the other between Larsen's legs on the seat.

Headlights startled her as a pickup truck parked nearby. Two men got out. The man on the passenger side saw them in the car. Amanda bent forward and slid on the wig. She leaned over and put her arms around Larsen, pulling his head up and pretending to kiss him. She heard the two men laugh as they walked inside the building.

Amanda turned the ignition key, and the engine started immediately. Sliding over so she could reach the gas pedal with her left foot, she put the car into reverse. She checked to make sure no other cars were occupied and backed across the parking lot.

When she reached the paved street she continued across into the parking lot of a NAPA auto parts store on the opposite side. She steered the car toward the glass storefront. On impact the large window shattered, sending chunks of glass and a shower of slivers through Larsen's open window like an ice storm. The tires squealed until the car stopped, halfway inside the storefront. Amanda was deafened by the store alarms.

Larsen's head hung out the open window, and specks of blood dotted his face where glass shards had pelted him. He looked like a passed-out drunk who'd bloodied himself in a wreck.

Amanda reached for her purse and removed the poultry shears. For a moment she imagined unzipping Larsen and doing what every mother in her place wanted to do. She hesitated, looking at the door handle. It's now or never. Amanda rose to her knees facing Larsen. His neck was limp as she rolled his head toward her to reach his left ear. Taking the bottom half of Larsen's ear between the blades of the shears, she clenched her teeth and squeezed. She shivered and almost vomited at the metallic click of the blades snapping closed. She wiped her sleeve across her lips and reached for the largest chunk of glass on the floor. In one quick motion Amanda sliced across the cut in Larsen's ear, deep into his cheek and down into his top lip, matching the angle of the scar on Pam's face. A river of blood raged down the left side of Larsen's face. She shoved his body back against the door, taking huge breaths to keep from gagging. She removed the earring, then tossed the broken glass and half an ear into Larsen's lap as she stepped out of the car.

The streetlight in the corner of the parking lot blinked off and on as Amanda rounded the building toward her car. She made herself walk at a normal pace. She wondered if Pam would like living in Panama City Beach. She hoped the movers arrived on time the next morning.

A Death in the Family

Through the large window, Red Mountain blocks the Birmingham sunset. Daylight above the trees fades from white to yellow. I hold mother's plastic pill bottle in my lap and stare over the horizon of hospital blanket covering her shriveled outline.

Mother hardly stirs for hours. I neither read nor watch television. She coughs, as she's done every few minutes for the past thirty hours, no louder than a kitten sneeze. I wonder how many other daughters up and down the hallway hold vigil alone this evening.

After a short visit on the way home from his office, my brother Bobby has left to check on his two sons, my two nephews, and to help his wife Molly get them fed and started on their homework. In the fifth and sixth grades, they are beginning to act and look like little men, different from the grown men in my life only in that they can't drive too fast or spend their money foolishly.

The doctor prescribed the pills. A huge orange bottle. For the pain, he said, but I know different. This is the way the doctors do it. With Mother's weak heart, even a small dose might let her go to sleep and never wake. I pray she won't wake up again, but not so much for her own peace. I cannot tolerate much longer her incessant begging for the doctor to "give me something and let me die."

I consider how to do it. Offer her a handful of pills and say go to it? Open a few capsules and sprinkle them into her milk? Smile and suggest one each time she awakens until her energy simply fades?

I'm not distraught that my mother is dying. She is 93, after all, and has suffered few hardships in her life, growing up in a family of means. No, I'm sad because I know my last memories won't be about hugs, parting words of love, or encouragement to carry on as the one she always knew would accomplish great things. I see no great future, but an end not unlike what I see before me. I will not enter the elite group of women who have so influenced our family, position gained through longevity and inheritance, not accomplishment.

My mental video replays her relentless begging to let her die. Or something meaningless. Her story of the bowl of coins Grandmother kept near the door during the Depression. For men who came knocking at the big house offering to rake leaves or clean gutters. Perhaps my last memory of her alive will be the look of contempt she flashes me in rare lucid moments.

In those last weeks when we actually conversed, before the last stroke, mother enjoyed reminding me daily of my three failed marriages. The other subject Mother relished: my child who offers me nothing but venom. Dear Sweet Alecia, the child without memory of the nights I held her tight and rocked her to sleep when her daddy didn't come home. Alecia, my late-in-life child the same as I was for Mother, God's answer to prayer. Alecia, who remembers only that last year she lived with me, when the only friends I kept were vodka and television movies until 4 a.m. When she fed herself cereal and walked to school, afraid to ride with me in my car with dents down the entire passenger side from mailboxes placed too close to the street.

Aunt Dorothy, Mother's younger sister, will be here in the morning for a last visit. The fourth so-called last visit in two years. Lord only knows if Mother will realize Aunt Dot is visiting. Mother occasionally swims to the surface of consciousness, just long enough to proclaim she wants to die. Yet she continues to grasp at the lifeboat for rescue which will not come.

I try to remember the time before the sickness that has consumed these last two years. I remember sitting in Aunt Dot's living room on my last visit to Atlanta. Nibbling almond crescent cookies. Sipping tea from bone china. Spode that Grandmother brought back from London on a luxury liner, one of her many trips across the Atlantic—though to my knowledge she never once flew anywhere. The conversation comes back to me. Aunt Dot teased that she still regretted Mother not marrying Travis Boyd from Chattanooga. Aunt Dot knows life would've been better for the family if Mother had done the right thing. "He was from the Livingston Boyds, you know, not the Taylor Boyds," she said, her crooked, arthritic finger pointed delicately upward for emphasis, never daring to actually point at someone, which would be terribly common and downright rude in her eyes. "That family came later. It was the *Livingston* Boyd family who had been truly prominent. His father's brother was a senator, you know."

****

I feel someone shaking my shoulder. It's Bobby, back after putting the boys to bed, reading the same story he read last night and the night before and many nights before that. He walks back to the door, flips the switch and the light pierces my eyes like electricity. I realize I'd dozed off, but the pills are still tight in my

hand. I slide them under my leg. Bobby shows no sign of noticing. "Go get some real sleep," he says, his voice tender, smiling as
I look up through blinking eyes. He's a good brother. The only
one who hasn't judged me and found me lacking in redeeming
qualities. I look at the white shroud that is what's left of Mother
and see she hasn't moved since rolling over a couple of hours earlier. She awakened once in the unlit room, only visible by the
light reflecting under the door, long enough to look me in the eye
and ask for the hundredth time this week to let her die. I experienced once again the opposite tugs of sympathy and disdain. I
understand how she feels.

"What time is it?" I ask Bobby, trying to rub the knot out of
my neck.

"Time for you to get out of here."

I realize I haven't been out of the hospital since yesterday as
I look down at my wrinkled blouse. Weeks ago I gave up on any
sort of normal routine. Daily baths and fresh clothes, meals at
noon and six, favorite television shows. I kiss Bobby on the
cheek and gather my sweater and purse. It's heavier than normal
with a pint of vodka, seal unbroken, tucked inside the zipper
pocket. For over two years I haven't had a drink, but last week I
found myself inside the package store adjoining the gas station,
placing the pint on the counter as I did thousands of times before
quitting.

Bobby and I step into the hall. We face each other in the
early light, which streams in and reflects on the polished tile cor-
ridor. We stand close. I see wrinkles beside his eyes, smile lines
that have somehow formed without me noticing, though neither
of us smiles.

"Bobby, I don't think I can do this any more."

"She asked about dying again?"

I lower my voice, knowing Mother often lies there listening with her eyes closed. "She's said nothing else to me. I read to her, but she just stared at the ceiling. When I finished, all she did was ask to see the doctor, so he would let her die. Then she rolled over with her back to me." I glance past his shoulder, through the door, before I finish. "I don't trust myself with her."

He looks at me, his expression revealing more disappointment than anger. He wipes his mouth, thinking. "You don't mean that."

I look into his eyes. I hold him that way and hope he can see deep inside me, hope he can tell me what I can't see: what's really there. I turn and walk out without speaking. What I want is a future in which there are no dreams, no memories of a husband holding 12-year-old Alecia's hand as he slams the front door behind them, causing me to spill my ice and vodka onto the carpet.

****

The door to my room in Bobby's house is kept closed. I see why. Everything in this room is robin's-egg blue, remnants of Bobby's first wife. The walls, two small vases on the bedside table, a throw on the rocking chair, the border of the small rug, even the lampshade. All blue. Appropriate color I tell myself, not bothering to laugh at my own joke. I switch on the small television on top of the chest and lay across the bed, not bothering to turn back the bed spread, blue of course.

After an hour of sleepiness without sleep, I stack the two pillows, prop myself to look up at the television and kick my shoes over the bedside. The bottle of pills presses uncomfortably into my thigh, but I leave it there as penance. I think of Alecia and wonder what a fifteen-year-old living in California might be doing on a cold night like this. If it's even cold in California. I wonder if she thinks of me, and if so, if I am still "Mother." I wonder if she would sit beside my bed some day as I lay weak and powerless, withered from a life alone, begging for the doctor to let me go. Sometime long after I see the orange clock numbers read 1:31 a.m. I dream of myself in bed with my mother, sweating where our arms and legs touch and create heat.

****

The hospital is quiet this morning. Not many visitors at six a.m. The halls are empty. Nurses hover near the counter like ghosts, sipping coffee, muttering quietly beneath the humming florescent lights.

I nudge Bobby and he smiles up at me. "You're back already?" he says, rubbing sleep from his eyes with his knuckles. He checks his watch. "I could have stayed until seven thirty."

When he's gone I wrap my shoulders in the thin caramel-colored blanket one of the nurses has folded over the back of the chair. I stare down at mother, who appears exactly the same as when I left. Her chest slowly rises and falls. I hear her tiny voice. She speaks without turning her head. "Why don't you find something useful to do? I don't need you here."

Nice to see you, too, Mother. I flop into my chair and pull the blanket over my legs. I slide my hand into my pocket and close my eyes. Soon I dream of opening pills and salting Mother's watery instant mashed potatoes, or somehow opening the drip bottle of clear fluid.

I wake when the nurse rolls the table over Mother for lunch and realize it's the longest sleep I've had in days. They've brushed Mother's hair and have her propped on pillows to feed her a small amount of green Jell-O and the mashed potatoes from my dream. I stare back at her flat, emotionless face and wonder how a mother can grow to so dislike a daughter, but then I think back on the past few years and know. I do know. I smile at Mother. My mind is clear now, and I am relieved. I'm not tired any more. And I'm in no hurry to get out of here, though I usually hate listening to her cough and choke as she tries to swallow. Today it doesn't bother me, and for the first time in weeks I sit through her entire lunch.

When the nurses leave I open the window, hoping for a breeze. I stand near Mother and run my hand gently through her hair and down her cheek. I do love her. And I always wanted to make myself worthy, but hours at the piano, numbing my fingers, and dreaded dance classes were never enough to overcome my poor sense of rhythm, to create the little star she wanted. For a moment I think of what my ex said when our daughter had skipped school. She just wants your attention, he'd yelled at me, as if it were all my fault she was caught with two older boys smoking pot.

Mother looks up at me wondering, questioning, uncertain. My other hand remains in my pocket, where I finger the pill bottle for comfort.

I sit back in my chair and wait, knowing she will soon fall asleep. She does. I slide the bottle from my pants pocket as I stand, shaking half of the pills into my palm.

From her pitcher on the bedside table, I pour a glass of cold water. I watch her face but see no pain.

I close my eyes and listen, breathing deeply, focusing on this moment. Nurses' shoes squeak in the hallway. Somewhere in the distance a car alarm sounds for a few seconds. I smell the pink blooms of the camellia bush near the window and open my eyes to watch them sway in the morning breeze. I look down at my upturned palm and know the time is right.

The taste is unexpectedly bitter.

Robert Earl and W.C.

Robert Earl turned the Coca-Cola bottle up to drain the last few swallows of Jim Beam bourbon and Coke. He and his brother W.C. had been passing the bottle back and forth on the drive home from fishing the spillway of the Claiborne Lock and Dam. Behind the two men a red ice chest with duct tape holding a cracked lid together, half full of channel catfish, slid from side to side of the truck bed whenever the road curved. Half a dozen Zebco 33 rods and reels dangled over the tailgate. Hooks and weights tangled in the wind and knotted around the rod tips.

W.C. took one hand off the steering wheel and reached toward Robert Earl. "Hey, save me a swallow," he said, realizing his request was too late even as he said it. W.C. aimed the truck tires at a pothole, which jarred the bottle between Robert Earl's lips and caused drops of brown liquid to dribble down both sides of his mouth.

"Dammit, W.C., can't you drive no better than that?"

W.C. didn't look over, forcing himself not to laugh. "I ain't the one made the roads."

"And you ain't the one paying no attention neither."

Robert Earl tossed the bottle onto the seat next to a brown paper sack holding the empty pint bottle. The cab of the new Dodge Ram truck grew quiet. Only the whir of the air condition-

er fan on high filled the void of sound. The brothers were comfortable with silence after logging hundreds of trips and thousands of miles in their work ferrying cars for Monroeville's big car
dealer. Even as kids they didn't feel every moment required conversation. They might sit side-by-side holding cane poles for an
hour without speaking, as a small pond near their house on the
edge of town.

Two minutes later, Robert Earl picked up the Coke bottle
and pushed the button to lower the passenger window. "Watch
this," he said, as he leaned halfway out the window and cocked
his arm, holding the green glass bottle high above his head.

W.C. glanced over at Robert Earl, whose thin gray-blond
hair was pinned back by the wind. Seeing the highway sign indi-
cating a crossroad ahead, W.C. knew the routine. He glanced
down and saw the needle just past eighty. He steered near the
side of the road and slowed to fifty. "This is a nice ride. I might
get me one of these if old Foster wasn't so damn proud of 'em."

W.C. watched as Robert Earl timed his release and flung the
bottle forward toward the sign. The expected explosion of glass
never came. The unbroken bottle ricocheted off the left edge of
the yellow and black sign into the middle of the truck's windshield. The bottle shot through a hole in the center of a spider-
ing pattern of cracks, glanced off the side of W.C.'s face and
smashed into the back window with a loud crack. A hailstorm of
glass pelted the inside of cab, and the wind whistled like a jet
engine through the hole in the windshield.

W.C. swerved the truck left and jammed his boot down on
the brakes with his eyes closed. The tires locked as the truck
crossed both lanes and came to rest in the ditch on the other side
in a cloud of black smoke. "Shit damn son of a bitch!" W.C yelled

as he turned off the ignition.

As a cloud of fine July dust drifted in front of the truck, W.C. looked over at Robert Earl and saw from his look that he was also uncertain what to do next. W.C. heard catfish flopping around in the back of the truck from the overturned ice chest. He brushed tiny pieces of glass from his hair and off the front of his blue work shirt. "Man, you could of got us killed or something. And that glass has cut me," W.C said, realizing blood was running down the side of his face, wetting his collar. "Damn you, Robert Earl."

"Well, we done it a thousand times and that never happened before. It weren't my fault."

"What are we going to tell Mr. Foster now? He doesn't even know I kept the extra keys after we delivered the truck yesterday. Look at that hole in the windshield. He's going to fire both our asses. My old lady said she'd kick me out if I come home again without a job, so you better get that couch ready."

As the shock of the crash wore off, W.C. touched the side of his face. He looked down at his t-shirt and saw the entire right side was turning red. "Good Lord, I must of got a deep cut. And it's getting all over the damn seat. How bad's it look? It's burning like a some bitch."

Robert Earl looked up at W.C.'s head and immediately threw up onto the seat between them.

"Godamighty, Robert Earl. What's wrong with you? Cain't you open a door if you got to puke?" W.C. yelled. He quickly slid away from Robert Earl, trying to keep the bourbon and Coke lunch remains off his pants. He reached up and touched the side of his head. His touch felt like he'd branded himself with a hot poker. "Now look at the side of my face and tell me what it looks like. I know I got a bad cut. So go on, how bad is it?"

Robert Earl wiped his mouth on the sleeve of his white t-shirt. He wanted to speak, but could think of no words that seemed appropriate. Instead of saying anything, he reached up to the back of the seat behind W.C. and picked up W.C.'s right ear between his thumb and finger and dangled the warm flesh for his brother to see. When W.C. realized what Robert Earl was holding, he vomited into the stinking puddle on the seat, dripping onto the floorboard.

****

Robert Earl tapped on the window of W.C.'s hospital room. He stood behind an overgrown privet hedge and hoped no one spotted him from the parking lot. Robert Earl saw W.C.'s gray braided ponytail as he lay on his side with his head turned away. Robert Earl tapped again, and W.C. sat up rubbing his eyes and looked at the door. W.C. still had the bandages wrapped around and around his head like a mummy, with a big mound of gauze over the ear that had been sewn back on. Robert Earl was proud he'd thought to stick the ear in a McDonald's cup and cover it with ice that had spilled into the back of the truck when the fish cooler turned over.

"W.C., let me in," Robert Earl half whispered, half yelled through the closed window. "I brought whiskey."

W.C. slowly put his feet over the side of the bed and stood up. His butt, white as paste and a perfect contrast to his back that had turned caramel-colored from fishing shirtless for the past half a century, showed through the hospital gown that didn't quite go all the way around. He shuffled to the doorway and looked both directions down the hall before shutting the heavy door and walking over to open the window. Robert Earl held out his hand, but W.C. simply reached through the window and took the grocery sack from his brother with the fifth of Jim Beam and two short Cokes, then walked back to the bed and sat down to open the bottle, ignoring the chaser.

Robert Earl mumbled "damn," then pulled himself up with both hands and hooked a leg over the metal sill, gasping as he clung there with the heel of one thick-soled black shoe keeping him from falling back to the ground. He wasn't sure how to swing himself on up and inside the room, so he just hung there with his skinny, almost hairless white leg sticking out from his pants. "Don't worry yourself none about me, W.C. You got a fine way of saying thank you." Straining and inching himself up, Robert Earl finally managed to fall through the opening. He sat on the floor huffing from the effort. "Like I said, I can climb in all by myself. I climbed my first tree over sixty years ago and didn't get your help then either, big brother."

W.C. poured three fingers of whiskey into a plastic cup, mulling what Robert Earl had said. He sipped the bourbon. "Well, at least this time you won't go running to Mama with a broken arm and getting my ass tanned for not watching out."

"You don't look like you need none of that," Robert Earl said, now reclining against the wall heater. He ignored his brother's dig. "I saw how you wobbled over to the door. What kind of pain pills they got you on?"

"They ain't worth a damn. I had Mepergan the first three days, but now I just got these Loratabs. You have to take two or three of the damn things just to get a buzz, so I have to hold them in my mouth until the nurse leaves and wait until I get three saved up. But this whiskey will help."

"Well just give me two then," Robert Earl said. He thought

he shouldn't be greedy, since W.C. was the one who had his ear sewed back on.

"Give you two? Do I look like a damn doctor?"

"I brought the whiskey; now give me one at least."

W.C. reached over for the Gideon's King James Bible sitting on his bedside and flipped it open. He found a pill in the middle of The Book of Revelations and tossed it to Robert Earl.

Robert Earl pushed himself up, walked to the bathroom, found a plastic cup, and poured himself half a glass of whiskey. "When I come out of the Piggly Wiggly buying a carton of smokes and a few groceries this morning, I saw old man Foster in that new truck we delivered. He had the windshield fixed. I was parked two cars over, so I stuck an Irish potato over his tailpipe after he went inside the Pig. I reckon that stopped him when he got a block or two."

"You don't think he saw your car?"

"I don't give a damn. He can't prove nothing. And he didn't have any right to fire us like that just for borrowing his damn truck. Nobody needed it on a Sunday."

W. C. laughed a little. "He may not of needed it on a Sunday, but I bet he didn't need no hole in the windshield nor puke neither. And you needn't rile him up more, or he won't ever hire us back."

"Hell W.C., think about it. For all he knew we were telling the truth about them boys throwing the bottle out from a car going the other way. They can't prove nothing just because they found a empty pint in the floorboard. And wrecks can make a lot of people throw up. It don't mean you're drunk."

"You right about that. We wasn't drunk on no pint."

Robert Earl tossed the last swallow of whiskey into the back of his throat and said, "It just ain't right to fire us without proving we done anything. We got rights you know." He picked up the TV remote to signal he'd said his piece, found the Atlanta Braves playing on TBS and turned the sound down low.

A few minutes later Robert Earl said, "Your old lady dropped off a box at my trailer with your clothes, that old Joe Namath bobble-head doll and a clock radio. She said that was all she had that was yours, but to call if you thought of something else."

W.C. nodded, said nothing.

Overhead, the florescent light hummed. The two men sat there sipping straight whiskey, watched the baseball game with the sound down and said nothing, until both fell asleep.

****

W.C. and Robert Earl enjoyed the unseasonably warm autumn afternoon as they rode north on Interstate 65 on the way back from Mobile to Monroeville. They'd delivered two used cars to a wholesaler for Mr. Foster and were returning in a new minivan. The windows were down, and each rested an arm on his door.

"How long you think we been ferrying cars to Mobile and back for old man Foster's dealership?" Robert Earl asked W.C., who had insisted on driving that day.

W.C. thought about it, ran his hand through his long hair and hooked a loose strand behind his ears. "I don't know. Eight or ten years?" W.C. reached to turn down the country music station that had been blaring over the commotion of wind.

"Ten years last month," Robert Earl said, as he slapped his thigh. "I just figured it out. Started right out after I early retired from the mill, and that was ten years ago."

"I'll be damn."

"We need to celebrate. Not many brothers get to work together for ten years. Hell, you never even stayed married that long."

W.C. scratched his chin. "Well, at least I had three women who would say yes, and two more that would have if they'd been able to get an outright divorce. That's a hell of a lot better than you did with just one wife, and a foreigner at that."

"She wasn't no foreigner, she was Puerto Rican and that's really just like a state. And don't be speaking ill of the dead no way," Robert Earl said, thinking of the wife he always spoke of as dead, though in fact he knew she was living in Chicago after running away with a long-haul trucker. "Look, there's a Chevron at this first Atmore exit that has a package store on the side of it. Pull off here, and I'll get us a pint." Robert Earl raised his hip and dug out his wallet. He opened it to pull out a bill and waved the money in front of W.C. "I got a ten. I'll buy. Come on, just a celebration nip."

"I don't think Foster would like it if he found us drinking on another delivery. He said no more chances. I think he means it this time." The memory of last time he and Robert Earl had been drinking and driving made him reach up to touch his ear. The soreness was a little better, he thought. He glanced in the mirror and saw the skin was still bright pink, shifting to deep purple in the stitching that circled the ear like a tiny railroad bed.

As the exit was nearing, Robert Earl took one last shot. "It's just a pint. That ain't going to hurt nothing. Ten years we been shuttling damn cars back and forth for Foster. Ten years. And what you got to show for it? At least we can have a drink for heaven's sake to take the edge off this lonesome road."

W.C. turned away from his brother, looking across the interstate to a wide pasture. Round hay bales cast long shadows across the freshly cut field. The smell of the drying hay filled the car with its toasty aroma, reminding W.C. of fall and college football on the radio and his childhood roaming the rolling hills around Monroeville with his younger brother in tow. The cedar trees along the fence rows stood still in the windless afternoon. He looked back at his brother for several seconds, then eased back on the accelerator and steered the truck down the exit toward the Chevron station.

The Consequence of Summer Heat

L
anny Pritchard watched from the hood of his Dodge Ram with his feet propped on the oversized bumper, curious about the small car with a Madison County license plate and a Greenpeace sticker. He also noticed a faded Cumberland Law School parking decal. A man and a woman walked toward him on the gravel driveway from the waterfall behind his cousin Eric's house, built near the bottom of a sheer rock cliff. Lanny eased down from where he'd been sitting after parking his truck to block the car's exit. There were few visitors in this north end of Paint Rock Valley, and Lanny rarely saw a car he didn't recognize. He failed to notice if the car was an Accord or a Camry or whatever, caring little for tiny foreign cars that all looked alike and seemed to come only in white or silver. He walked forward and stopped between the couple and their car.

Lanny reached into the side pocket of his jeans to retrieve a flint arrowhead. "I found this point just over in the field," he stated, looking down at the two as he held the arrowhead up between the thumb and finger of his left hand. "They say that waterfall was an Indian trading site."

He spoke to the woman with black hair tied in a pony tail. She had the look he loved: sleek hair, smooth skin, a hint of

111

freckles across her cheeks, rosy from the brisk wind. And no makeup. She was in her mid twenties. Thirty tops.

"I'm Elizabeth. This is John," she said, holding out her hand, which Lanny shook.

"Lanny." He took care not to squeeze, but he need not worry. Her grip felt strong, confident. Lanny did not offer his hand to John, instead extending the arrowhead toward the woman.

Elizabeth cut her eyes toward John as she reached for the piece of stone.

Lanny dropped the arrowhead into her upturned palm. "It's real. They surface in the field after a big rain when it's freshly plowed."

The woman focused on the finely worked edges of the symmetrical stone. A few loose strands of her dark hair blew across her face. She tucked the hair behind her ear.

"Do you know Eric?" she asked. "You must be a neighbor?"

John stepped to her side and looked down at the arrowhead. "That's a nice one," he said.

Lanny almost laughed as the man attempted to inject himself into the conversation, all the while glancing over his shoulder down the road, probably hoping Eric would drive up.

Lanny saw Elizabeth's face flush. He was unsure if it was her boyfriend's lame attempt to step up or if she'd seen his eyes sweep across her body.

"I guess you're a friend of Eric's?" John asked.

"Yeah, sure. I know everybody up here in the Valley," Lanny said.

Back near the waterfall, high above cedar trees lining the top of a sheer limestone drop-off, crows began a high-pitched wailing as mockingbirds dipped and dived at the crows, chasing their larger black enemies from their nests in the trees.

"My cabin's tucked into that draw," Lanny said, tilting his head toward a cedar-sided cabin with a green metal roof at the far edge of a field. A row of towering sweet gum trees screened the front of the house, their broad leaves turning over with each gust. The rich reddish earth had been plowed into parallel lines that curved with the crescent shape of the field. Tiny ribbons of green corn stalks four or five inches tall topped the furrows.

"You can have that point," Lanny said to Elizabeth.

"Oh no, I couldn't," she said, holding the stone out. "It's too nice."

He left his hands in his pockets. She returned an uncomfortable smile.

"I have a hundred like it," he said.

She continued to hold out the flint.

Lanny reached for the flint piece, closing his thick hand around hers for a moment, allowing her to feel his strength.

Elizabeth pulled her hand back as if she'd touched a hot coal. Lanny chuckled. "Didn't mean to startle you."

"Well, I guess Eric's not around," John said, taking a step toward the car. "We better get back to the campground before dark. Tell Eric that John and Lizzy stopped by."

Lanny saw something flash across Elizabeth's face as John called her Lizzy and mentioned the campground.

"What's the hurry, Lizzy? Can I call you Lizzy?" Lanny said in response. His eyes were locked with hers. Then he looked over his shoulder at the sun glowing like a house fire in the oak and hickory trees along the high ridge running west. "It's an hour before dark. Eric might be along soon."

****

Lizzy forced a smile. Lanny made her uncomfortable, and there was no reason to tell him they were camping nearby. The Paint Rock Campground was the only public camping in the area. Lanny would know that. Then she felt silly. Obviously he was some friend of Eric, though she wondered why Eric had never mentioned him. She tried to look anywhere but into the eyes of the muscular man standing in front of her, his forearms revealing ropes of muscle beneath tanned skin.

She wished she'd called Eric ahead of time, instead of trying to surprise him. Eric had been her lab partner in college for two semesters. They remained friends even after the night of two bottles of wine, when she slept with him, then confessed the next morning that she really didn't have that kind of feeling for him. "Why can't you just let it be what it was, Eric? What's wrong with an intimate moment among friends?" she'd asked, as if everyone could turn their feelings on and off the way she could. She learned that Eric's temper matched his thick red hair when he pounded his fist on the bed and left without saying anything, slamming the front door hard enough to rattle pictures on the wall.

As she expected, he called an hour later. She accepted his apology, but not before she told him, "You scared me, Eric. I've never seen that side of you." In her mind, she could still see the fury she'd never imagined could come from blue eyes so vivid they sparkled like chipped ice. Neither of them had ever mentioned that episode again.

Since then, Lizzy had a brief marriage that began in her final semester of law school and ended when the dishwasher sat in pieces on her kitchen floor for six months, her husband promising to fix it every week as a point of pride, refusing to let her call a repairman. She moved back home alone, two hours north to Huntsville, and buried herself in her new job with a downtown corporate law firm.

It was hard to say what had changed in her life, or what happened to her promise to herself to control her own future, but she had let John gradually transform a friendship into a casual romance.

Today she was seeing another side of John. He stood straighter than usual and his voice sounded a bit deeper. Earlier, he'd seemed relieved that Eric was not home. Men behaved so funny around other men.

For six months, John had been living with her. The long hours writing briefs for the senior partners had made it impossible to date, even after she felt like getting out into the world again. Eric had called many times and even wrote sweet letters of encouragement during her divorce, but John—a friend since high school—was there every day. He'd won her over by being close with a glass of wine and a hand to hold through the year of guilt, anger and loneliness as she faced the failure of her marriage.

John and Lizzy both liked hiking and camping, and rarely did a cross word pass between them. Without really discussing moving in, she realized one day his shirts were hanging in her closet and he had his own drawer at her house. She had already admitted to herself that she didn't like living alone. When his apartment lease came up, they agreed he should move to her house. But already, as much as she dreaded the answer, she had asked herself if the situation with John was a relationship of convenience.

Her first impression of Lanny as he'd slid off the hood of this truck had been redneck farmer; now he stood so straight she thought *soldier*. His clean-shaven face was wrinkle-free. A strong jaw line defined a face with intense dark eyes.

"John's right," she told Lanny, "We need to get moving. Please tell Eric we'll try to stop by later."

She stepped around Lanny toward the driver's side of the Mazda. "Nice to meet you, Lanny. Can you back over to the side and let us through?"

He smiled, showing teeth so white she had to stare. *Bleach. He bleaches his teeth.*

****

Lanny noted he'd been right that the girl was the driver. Maybe she was the lawyer, too.

"Eric should be back soon. Why don't we just get a couple of beers and wait? I picked up a twelve-pack on the way back from town. It's iced down in the truck."

Lanny walked behind them to the truck. He dug through the ice and pulled out three Bud Lights, placing them on the tailgate. "Come on now," he said, in a loud but friendly tone. "Have one beer and see if Eric shows up."

Lanny knew that Eric was vacationing in Gulf Shores and not due back until late that evening, but the girl intrigued him. He held up two beers in his fists. "Good and cold."

Lanny saw the man's shoulders slump. The girl glared at her friend, obviously expecting him to say something. But neither spoke. Lanny stood there holding a beer in each hand with his arms up, as if he were waiting for his best buddies. "Eric will be pissed at me if I don't take care of his friends. One beer. Come on."

Lanny saw she didn't like him delaying them there, but neither she nor John would say so.

John spoke first, "One beer, Lanny, then we really have to move on. We want to get up early to hike the Walls of Jericho."

The woman's eyebrows rose and her mouth opened slightly, but she held her thoughts. John closed the car door he'd been holding open. Lanny knew the couple's ride back to the campground would be unpleasant.

The two walked back toward Lanny standing behind the truck tailgate and accepted the beers, each of which Lanny opened one-handed as he held the cans out. The laughter of crows echoed down through the cove behind the house as they darted through the trees, teasing their pursuers. Lanny opened a beer for himself. "To your health," he said. He tilted the can and drained half of it.

****

The sunset faded and darkness draped the circle of trees lighted by their campfire. Lizzy sat on a hard plastic ice chest with her elbows propped on her knees, watching the tip of orange flame writhing above the twig and broken stick fire. Smoke curled and hung there between Lizzy and John. Crickets, frogs, and pops from the fire provided background. The thick limbs of white oaks filled with half-grown bright leaves formed a ceiling, but she could glimpse a few stars through openings.

John sat on the opposite side of the fire and poked at the coals with a crooked stick. Sparks rose in the smoke and drifted toward Lizzy's legs.

"Do you have to do that?" she asked. She knew she'd sounded critical and should apologize. She hated it when she caught herself being petty, and part of her wanted John to be man enough to throw her words back in her face, to somehow defend against her verbal jab. She'd never heard him raise his voice. Maybe computer programmers are just that way, she thought. Spending days tussling with a machine instead of a person and nights killing monsters in a cyber universe doesn't build conversational skills.

John looked through the hovering smoke at Lizzy, then tossed the stick into the fire without speaking.

They sat that way for a long time. Lizzy walked to the tent and kneeled to rummage through their cardboard box of food and drink. She pulled out a bottle of wine and a corkscrew.

"I'll get that for you," John said, sounding urgent. She knew this was his way to move past the argument they'd had in the car and the tension hovering over their camp like the smoke drifting too slowly into the trees.

Lizzy sipped her wine and returned to the fire, standing with her back to feel the heat. John relaxed in his folding chair with his legs extended and crossed at the ankles. Despite the warm spring days that hinted summer was near, the night air felt cool.

"Can we go by Eric's again tomorrow?" Lizzy asked. "He said he'd show you that new cave they found."

"Whatever you want is fine, but I was thinking more about the Walls," he said. "Do you think that weird guy will be at Eric's?"

"He wasn't so bad. He just has poor social skills." Lizzy wanted to bite her tongue. Why was she being so confrontational? She turned and slid the end of a tree limb farther into the fire with the toe of her hiking boot.

"Poor social skills? Hell, Lizzy, he practically held us hostage."

Lizzy felt guilt for enjoying the way John resented the man they'd met in Eric's driveway but found herself teasing him anyway. "Come on John, all he did was offer us a beer and try to get us to wait for Eric."

The woods grew quieter around them as they drank their wine from plastic cups and listened to the hiss of green wood sizzling over a bed of coals. Lizzie heard leaves rustle and the muffled crack of a twig.

"Did you hear that?" she asked, thinking she'd heard a footstep in dry undergrowth.

****

Not until the tent canvas glowed golden in the morning sunlight did Lizzy realize she had finally fallen asleep. She sat up in her sleeping bag blinking away the sleep and rubbed the back of her neck. She had lain there long into the night, listening to John snore quietly, trying to decide if she was really happy. Is this all she wanted? A comfortable relationship, hikes on the weekend and a job that paid well?

She heard a lone cardinal whistle from nearby and tiny peeps from a flock of sparrows right above her as they fluttered from limb to limb. John slept on his side, his face flat against a folded shirt he used as a pillow and his eyes closed. Lizzy wondered what had awakened her.

A car door slammed nearby. Pebbles crunched underfoot. Only in panties, she was not ready to meet a park ranger. She reached for her jeans and a thin short-sleeved yellow shirt, then nudged John's shoulder.

"John, someone's here."

He made a grunting sound but didn't move.

Lizzy unzipped the sleeping bag and lay on her back, hoisting her legs in the air as she slid the jeans on. She buttoned the shirt almost to the top, careful to cover the tiny chameleon lizard tattoo on her left breast. She ran her fingers through her hair. A bright yellow wedge of sunlight sliced into the tent as she pulled the tent zipper up, causing John to roll over and throw his arm over his eyes.

Lizzy stepped out, expecting a park ranger. She immediately recognized the big Dodge truck. She glanced around and saw Lanny squatting on his haunches, picking at the remnants of the campfire with a stick. He looked comfortable, as if he belonged there. His tight pants revealed the muscles in his legs.

"Morning," Lanny said, rising effortlessly to his feet, showing her the smile she knew he understood would turn most girls' heads. Lanny's smile was almost too perfect, too practiced, and were it not for the tiniest gap between his front teeth, she might give it a ten.

Lizzy glanced back into the tent. John sat up rubbing his eyes.

"What are you doing here?" she asked Lanny.

"I had to pass by this way to check a tract of timber my company's looking at. Thought I'd check on you Scouts."

"Well, we're fine. Did you tell Eric we came by?" A cool breeze caused the hair on her neck to stand up, and she remembered she was wearing a thin shirt and no bra. She reached into the tent for a sweatshirt and pulled it over her head.

"Yeah, he knows you're here. I told him you were camping and hiking the Walls today. I went by his house this morning to see if he wanted to come by here with me, but he was already gone. Figured he might be here."

John emerged from the tent, zipping his pants as he stepped

out barefoot, with no shirt. Although the sun was nearly topping the trees, he wrapped his arms around himself as if for warmth in the cool, misty air. His hair stuck out in every direction.

"Hey Sport," Lanny asked. "How'd you sleep?"

"You always wake people up this early?" John asked, as he rummaged through a knapsack for a shirt.

"It ain't that early. I thought you guys could use some coffee." He gestured with his thumb toward a large Thermos bottle on a rock near the fire pit.

A stack of Styrofoam cups was wedged over the top. Lizzy relaxed a little, seeing the coffee. She shrugged. "Well, I could use some."

****

"I don't like that guy any better today. He's creepy," John said as soon as Lanny had backed up his truck and started down the road. "Who goes to someone's camp like that when he hardly knows them?"

Lizzy didn't reply. She felt the same way. And she was thinking of the sounds she'd heard in the woods last night, like someone walking. John had convinced her that the sound was probably an armadillo. She leaned back in a folding chair, her feet propped on the ice chest, sipping black coffee. There was something about Lanny, but he didn't exactly fit the stereotype of the potbellied country boy in a bad movie. His hair was neatly cropped and short, his face clean-shaven, his shirts pressed. A muscular chest proved he was not afraid of work. He had strong legs, which attracted her. He couldn't be all that bad. After all, he'd done nothing except offer them beer and coffee.

"What do you think?" John pressed, after she ignored his first comment.

"You're probably right, but maybe he's really just trying to be hospitable," Lizzy said, as she lifted a cardboard box onto the small metal table. She removed a loaf of whole wheat bread and spread peanut butter on one slice, adding honey over the top. "Want one?" she asked, holding up the bread before taking a bite.

"Yeah." John walked to the table and stood there as Lizzy prepared a second slice. "Have you decided if you'll go with me to the Walls of Jericho?"

"I don't know," Lizzy answered. "They say it's quite a climb back up the new trail. I don't know if I'm up to it." She'd been there once, making the hour and a half hike on the original path into the cove to see the limestone cliffs before a shorter trail had been cut from the top side by the Nature Conservancy. "It's an incredible site, but I don't know. I'm not really feeling it."

"Yeah, figures."

"What do you mean?"

"You're just acting weird," John said, putting his hands in his pockets and shrugging.

Lizzy turned her head and looked at John for a long moment. The words *passive-aggressive* came to mind. She handed him the bread and walked off toward the creek with her coffee. The woods were now fully awake. In the distance she heard crows and the whine of tires on asphalt. The wind shifted to come from the creek bottom that bordered the campground, bringing with it the faint odor of a dead animal, a decay long past rancid and now almost sweet smelling as it mixed with the fragrance of six-inch, blooming bluebells that covered the shady slope below their tent.

When Lizzy returned from a short walk, John had tidied up

the camp site, washed their dishes and sat lacing his hiking boots, an open backpack near his feet. She could see a bottle of water and his camera. She emptied her pockets of trash she gathered on her walk: two crushed beer cans, a plastic bread bag and a fast-food wrapper from someone's hamburger.

"You're going to the Walls, I guess," Lizzy said. "So visiting Eric is out?"

"Yeah. Why don't you come with me" John asked. He stood and slung the pack over one shoulder. "We can run by Eric's afterward."

She shook her head in response. "So you're just leaving me here without a car?"

"They say the new path down only takes an hour. You can drop me off and come back later if you want."

****

Lizzy had driven the short distance into Tennessee almost to Winchester and cut over toward Belvedere, where she visited the wood-working shop with hand-crafted boxes she collected. On the seat beside her sat her new cedar jewelry box. The tight fit of the joints and the inlaid white wood in a diamond design on the top appealed to her as she ran her hand over the smooth surface.

Lizzy listened to the hum of the tires as she wound down the continuous curve of pavement that ran south from Huntland back into Alabama. She had the windows down to enjoy the warming air, a hint of the approaching summer she so craved. A country music station blared on the radio, above the whistle of the windows. She sang along with the songs she knew and made up words for the others.

After the turn at Swaim, Lizzy drove back up the mountain

and looked out over the small farms in the valley. Bright green grassy fields contrasted with stands of deep green cedar lining the fence rows. As she neared a long stretch of straight highway before the turn-in for the hiking trail, she noticed a dark pickup truck pulling away from the parking area a half a mile ahead.

She checked her watch. Twenty minutes early. She parked in the small gravel lot prepared for hikers visiting the landmark known as the Walls of Jericho, a place almost spiritual to many hikers, with rock walls forming a bowl shape that gives the feeling of entering a huge cathedral. She stepped out of the car and strolled around the clearing. Trash littered the edges of the lot, out of place amongst the wild mustard blooms of bright yellow that grew in patches along the near-white limestone rocks that had been placed as a border for the parking lot. She was even more disappointed when she thought about how even the hikers had ignored the trash in their eagerness to get down the trail and take pleasure in the outdoors. For the second time that day she found herself picking up other people's mess and dropping beer cans and paper into a large trash container. When she finished, she sat on a large flat outcropping of rock just down the trail and stretched her arms over her head. She locked her fingers together, made a box shape, then slowly pushed her hands as high as possible in a pose she'd learned in yoga class. She breathed in through her nose, noting the sharp scent of the nearby cedar, and exhaled slowly through her mouth.

Venturing a short way down the path, she bent to look at a patch of trillium, running her finger along one of the variegated leaves. Ferns grew along a steep embankment and were just beginning to unroll their long stems. Hen bit showed a few tiny purple blooms. She sat down with her back to a giant cedar and waited, the tree's carpet of dried, rust-colored needles forming a soft cushion.

Half an hour later she glanced at her watch. One in the afternoon. She calculated the time and knew John would be back soon if he hadn't stayed too long at the bottom of the mountain before starting the climb back up. She had not been down this new trail that entered from the top, but they had heard the walk was less than an hour. When she had made the hike years before with her soon-to-be husband, they had entered from the old trail at the other end of the cove, a longer walk but not as steep.

Lizzy walked back to the car for a bottle of water. The sun had passed the mid-point in the sky. She sat in the Mazda and turned on the radio. Another half hour passed. Lizzy saw from the dash clock she'd been waiting over an hour. She needed to pee. Her fingers drummed the seat beside her. John could be so inconsiderate.

Lizzy looked into the back seat and spotted the Huntsville newspaper from the day they had left, still rolled up in rubber band. She reached for the paper and began reading from the front page. Iraq news of bombings, fights in Congress over how judges are appointed or fired, scores dead in a Russian mine blast. She scanned the headlines and moved to the next page for something to hold her interest. Her horoscope told her that to have a great friend she must be a great friend. Just what I need, she thought. Another friend instead of a lover. She finished with the comics page.

Still no John.

She turned back to the front page and forced herself to read the articles she'd skipped the first time.

Lizzy looked at the clock again. John really was being unfair to make her wait like this. She opened the door and walked to the edge of the trail, peering as far down the mountain trail as possible. Nothing moved. She considered leaving, but then she would just have to make the twenty-five minute drive back up here. She walked a few feet into the woods and squatted to pee behind a large cedar, screening her from the road, though no cars had passed for half an hour.

As another hour passed, Lizzy began to imagine all the excuses John would make. The Walls were farther than they'd heard, he'd say. Or the cliffs were so gorgeous he'd lost track of time. Or he'd twisted his ankle. She sat up in her seat. What if John had twisted his ankle? Or worse? What if he'd broken a bone or something? She looked at her watch. Should she try to find him?

Half an hour passed. Lizzy walked to the trail head again. She looked around. No one. Only an occasional car had passed in the three hours she'd waited. The word desolate came to mind. She thought of the accused mass murderer who allegedly buried his victims all over a mountain just minutes away in Estill Fork, and she tried to remember what had ever happened in that case. Clothing was found buried, but the bodies weren't discovered, she thought. She looked out over the vista of valley and mountains, where not a single house could be seen from where she stood. If someone wanted to be undisturbed for something like that and needed secluded spaces to hide bodies, this would be the place.

She called out John's name. Then louder. Nothing. The sun descended its arc toward the trees.

Lizzy fought the panic building in the back of her head. She decided to go ask Eric to come back and help her find John. He must have wandered off the trail or something. He must be lost. She shouted his name one last time, then backed a wide circle in the parking area and drove toward Eric's house, hoping she would not run into Lanny.

Lizzy rubbed her sleeve over her eyes as she turned onto Highway 27 in front of Eric's house. She had begun to imagine John wandering in the woods and being lost overnight. She'd even allowed herself to think the worst and wondered if she would be in charge of funeral arrangements if John died. Or would John's mother take over? She needed to quit thinking like that, she told herself. She blamed herself for not going on the hike and keeping him on the trail.

Relief surged when she saw Eric standing in his front yard with a garden hose, watering a row of what appeared to be newly planted trees, apple, or maybe pear. She parked behind his truck and walked toward him through the long shadows the trees cast in the late afternoon light.

"Hello Great Counselor and Defender of Corporate Greed," Eric said, dropping the hose and holding out his arms to hug Lizzy. "I went by the campground this afternoon. Why didn't you tell me you were coming out?"

"I'm so glad you're home," Lizzy said, trying to smile.

"Something's wrong?"

"Probably not, but John hiked into the Walls of Jericho. He was already three or four hours late when I left the parking lot. Can you help me go look for him?"

Eric dropped the hose and walked over to turn the water off. "You're sure about the time? He knew you were waiting?"

"He said three hours. That was this morning."

"Let's get my cousin and ride back up there. I bet John's there waiting. It's so easy to lose track of time hiking down that trail."

"Your cousin?"

"You know Lanny. He moved into the cabin I built," Eric said, pointing toward the house. "He told me he met you."

"We met Lanny, but he didn't mention he was your cousin. You never told me you had a cousin up here," she said as she tucked her hair behind her ears. "Are you sure we need him?"

"He's a real outdoors guy. When he got back from two years in Iraq and quit the Marines, I rented him the house," Eric said. He placed his arm around Lizzy's shoulder as they walked side by side. "I'm sure everything is fine with John, but if he twisted his ankle or something Lanny could be a real help."

As the three arrived at the top side of the hiking trail, the sun changed from yellow to orange and dropped behind the trees, leaving the deep cove below them in shadow. Lanny had driven his truck, following Eric and Lizzy, and now motioned Eric over. Lizzy walked to the trail and yelled John's name twice, then returned to where Eric and Lanny stood. The woods lay quiet in the approaching twilight.

Lanny opened his truck box and removed two flashlights, handing one to Lizzy. Eric pulled a small flashlight from his pocket and pushed the switch.

"Light's almost gone. I can move a lot quicker by myself," Lanny said. "I think you two should stay here and call out to John once in awhile, in case he's lost. I'd like to get as far down as possible before pitch dark, but that's only about half an hour."

Lizzy looked at Eric.

Eric nodded. "He's probably right. Let's you and me just wait here."

"If you think so," Lizzy said. She slid her hands into her jeans pockets, feeling a slight chill as the temperature dropped in the fading light.

"I'll be back as soon as I can," Lanny said over his shoulder as he started off at a trot down the steep trail. She heard the rocks on the trail crunch rhythmically beneath Lanny's boots until the sound faded into the dark.

Lizzy sat on one of the large rocks lining the edge of the parking area. Every few minutes she stood and yelled down the side of the mountain. She honked the car horn once, but its blare on the otherwise quiet mountain was too unnatural and only increased her sense of dread.

Shadows ran together as the sunlight dimmed. In fifteen minutes the nearly full moon lit the parking lot and tree line. Her eyes adjusted to the evening light. Eric sat beside her. He tried to start a conversation a few times, but she offered only one-word answers to his questions and comments.

Lizzy called to John from where she sat, not bothering to walk to the edge of the trail. Then she heard footsteps on the path. She jumped to her feet uncertain if she should be mad or thrilled to see John. "John?"

"It's me. Lanny."

Eric stood. "You didn't find John?"

As Lizzy walked toward Lanny, she could see him studying her face. The moon had now risen high above the trees. Even without a flashlight, she could see sweat tracking down the sides of his face. He did not smile.

"What, Lanny? What is it?" she asked. She stepped closer and put her hand out to grip Lanny's arm. She could see the strained look on his face. She feared what he had to say.

"It's your friend. I found him below the trail at the bottom of a cliff. I'm sorry, he's dead."

She wanted to argue, to ask if maybe he was just unconscious, to check herself. But she let Lanny take her hand. The look in his eyes and his gentle touch told her he knew for certain.

****

Lizzy sat in the back of the sheriff's car with the door open and a thin wool blanket around her shoulders. Her head was down, but she wasn't crying. Her fingers locked together in her lap.

Blue and red lights flashed through the trees from the sheriff's car, a rescue truck from the Skyline fire department, and an ambulance from Scottsboro. A dozen people, mostly men dressed in camo or jeans and flannel, milled around the area, standing in small groups. Now and then a two-way radio strapped to a fireman's belt broke the silence. He would mutter a few words into the black box before placing it back on his hip. Lizzy looked at her watch. Nearly two in the morning.

Eric walked to car and leaned down, bracing himself with his hand on the car's roof and speaking softly. "I see several flashlights coming up the trail. I think they may be bringing John out."

Lizzy swung her legs out of the car and rose, keeping the blanket robed around her. "I want to see him."

"I don't think that's such a good idea."

Lizzy just stared. "I have to see him, Eric." She pushed past him as she saw four men carrying a metal stretcher with a body covered by a blanket just like the one she wore.

The sheriff held out his hand to signal to the men bearing the stretcher to stop. "Ma'am, you don't have to see the body. Mr. Pritchard said he had met Mr. Vance, and he's already identified the body. There was a wallet in his pocket with his driver's license. I'm very sorry."

"What happened?" Lizzy asked, still staring at the brown blanket.

"He was at the bottom of a real steep place below the trail. Looks like he was climbing over near the edge and must have slipped."

"I need to see him," she said, taking a step closer. The men all looked at the sheriff, who nodded. They eased the stretcher to the ground.

The sheriff knelt opposite Lizzy and pulled the blanket back enough to show the face.

Lizzy put her hand to her mouth, seeing John's face swollen and smudged with dirt, very pale, blood crusted around his nostrils.

"That's him, ma'am? You are confirming that's John Vance?" the sheriff asked.

Lizzy nodded. The sheriff pulled the blanket gently over the face. When Lizzy turned to walk away, she realized how quiet the parking lot had become. Everyone had stopped whatever they were doing and stood still, watching her. She pulled the blanket tighter around her shoulders and spun around, uncertain where to turn, where to go. Trees circling the parking area pulsed red and blue.

Someone behind her held her shoulders and led her with large, firm hands over to lean against the closed back door of the sheriff's car. She leaned into a shoulder as she felt an arm around her. *Eric*, she thought. She lay her head on his shoulder. Just as she did, she glimpsed up and realized the man offering comfort was Lanny.

****

Eric watched Lizzy sort through the purse in her lap for her glasses so she could read the Garden Delight menu. She was thinner, he noted, but it defined the chiseled beauty of her face more than ever. He said nothing. He smiled at her across the small steel table, a concrete sidewalk beneath their feet.

Eric heard the waiter, but did not look away from Lizzy. He was determined that this moment, this date, would be perfect for Lizzy to realize how much he cared for her. He'd been patient, and nothing would make him lose focus now. She turned toward the waiter as he placed glasses of water in front of them with lemon wedges floating on top.

"Hi, I'm Albert. I'll be right back to get your orders. Our lunch specials are on the chalk board near the door. Any questions about the menu?"

"No, thanks Albert," Eric said, still without looking up.

Eric slid his chair forward a couple of inches and leaned toward Lizzy with his elbows on the table. "I'm glad you could have lunch," he said, picking up the menu. "I like the new do, by the way."

"Thanks. I haven't had it cut this short since I was ten." Lizzy ran her hand through her cropped hair, which immediately sprang back exactly as it had been.

Eric watched Lizzy look over the menu, but she seemed distracted and uninterested.

"I'm glad you kept calling," she said. "It's been too long."

He just nodded, telling himself to be easy-going.

The early spring breeze was cool, but the clear sky let the sun warm them enough to sit outside. The two studied their menus for a minute before the waiter returned.

"I'll just have the salad with the baby greens and grilled chicken breast. With your raspberry vinaigrette." Lizzy said, handing her menu to the waiter. "And a glass of unsweet peach iced tea."

"The same," Eric said.

After Albert left the table, Eric gazed at Lizzy. "You're a hard lady to pin down. Thanks for having lunch with me."

"I'm sorry I haven't called back. I do appreciate all the calls and the little emails to check on me," Lizzy said.

"Not a problem. You're here now. You doing all right?"

Lizzy looked away. She picked up her napkin and spread the thin paper across her lap before answering, smoothing the edges over her legs. He waited, not pushing her to answer, seeing she was uncomfortable.

"Eric, let's talk about you. I'm so tired of talking about me. I'm fine. Let's leave it at that." The words hung in the air like a startled bird.

Eric avoided showing any sign on his face other than contentment to be with her. "Not much to say. Work is about the same." He leaned forward a few more inches, his voice softer as he spoke. "Lizzy, I had a reason for calling so much."

"What do you mean?" she asked.

"I know it's been rough. But life has to go on. It'll soon be a year. Can I take you out for dinner? A real date?" Eric asked, tilting his head slightly to the right and trying to hold her eyes with his. "I understand if it's too soon. But you must know how I feel about you."

A gust blew from behind Lizzy, and Eric saw her shiver slightly. Must be her new short hair. Or maybe that blue jean skirt—the shortest he'd ever seen her wear.

Lizzy reached over and took his right hand in both of hers.

"Eric, we've been down that path before," she said, then shifted in her chair. She looked uncomfortable. "Have you talked to Lanny lately?"

Eric pulled his hand back casually as he sat straight in his chair. "That's a question, not an answer," he said, forcing a chuckle and regretting it immediately. He hoped his forehead was not turning blotchy and red.

"So you haven't talked to him, have you?"

"He's made himself scarce the past few months. He moved back into town."

Eric tore a yellow packet of sweetener in half and stirred the powder into his tea. His mind was leaping ahead. Why would she bring up Lanny? He had not been expecting her words, and he could see where this was headed. He could feel his jaw muscles working.

"Well, in a way it's an answer," Lizzy said, fiddling with the plastic straw as she talked. "We've been dating."

****

Lizzy held the phone at arm's length as Eric talked and squeezed it before she put it back to her ear. She took a deep breath to calm herself, then spoke quietly. "Look, you've attacked Lanny every time we've talked for the last few weeks. Why are you so sure this is wrong?"

Eric's voice came back broken and scratchy on his cell phone, "Lizzy, there's still a lot you don't know about him."

"You keep saying that, but he's told me everything," Lizzy said as she sat on the swing on her front porch and let her shoes drop to the painted wooden floor. Even though the swing had been a birthday gift from her ex-husband, it was still her favorite spot at home. "He told me all the awful things he had to do in the war. I know how his wife killed herself running her car off a bridge and that's why he volunteered to go to combat. You haven't said one thing that he hasn't told me about."

Eric said something that was impossible to hear over the static.

"What? I can't hear you very well. You must be driving up the valley," Lizzy said.

She heard Eric's voice grow louder for a few seconds, though it sounded like he was wadding up paper while he talked. "Just ask him about his ring collection."

Before Lizzy could ask what he meant, the call dropped. She pressed the off button and laid the phone on the swing beside her. Long shadows from the neighbor's trees shaded her entire front porch. She looked at her watch and saw it was nearly six-thirty. Lanny would be home soon.

****

After a dinner of pepperoni pizza Lanny had picked up on his way home from work, Lizzy sat opposite Lanny on the couch listening to Lucinda Williams moaning about love gone wrong in South Mississippi. Lanny was finishing his fourth beer, while Lizzy sipped her first glass of merlot.

"I talked to Eric again this afternoon," Lizzy said, turning sideways on the couch and placing her feet in Lanny's lap. "Since I told him about us, he's gone off the deep end. He's really jealous."

"After we started seeing each other I couldn't find a good way to tell him. He talked about you all the time," Lanny said. He drained his beer, crushed the can completely flat in his hands and placed the metal disk on a leather coaster. "I dreaded the day he'd find out, but by then he'd almost stopped speaking to me anyway. That's why I moved back to town."

Lanny held one of Lizzy's feet and rubbed the sole, digging his thumbs into her arches.

"Mmmmm, that feels good. He talked about me all the time? So what did he say?"

"Eric is the closest family I have outside my mom," Lanny said, ignoring her question.

"I'm not sure how close he'll be now," Lizzy said, as if she were joking. For a few seconds they both considered the truth of what she'd said.

Lanny began massaging Lizzy's other foot. "I'll try to talk to him," he said. "He'll get over it." He reached over to unbutton the top button on her blouse, something she had grown to enjoy. She ignored him, allowing him to move down to the next button. He opened her blouse and ran his finger across the lizard tattoo on her breast.

"There's one thing," Lizzy said, trying to sound casual. "He said something about a collection of rings you had. What's that about? I'm just curious."

Lanny leaned back. His lips were pressed together, a sign she had learned meant that he was angry. "That's just something from my days in combat. Something I told him in confidence. It's nothing you need to worry about."

Lizzy took a deep breath, working to keep her voice at its normal pitch. "Well you can tell me in confidence, too. I'm not worried. It's just the whole thing sounds so mysterious."

Lanny stood, not answering. "You want some more wine? I'm grabbing a beer."

She shook her head. She started to say something about him

having his fifth beer on a work night, but thought better of bringing it up. She watched as he walked to the adjacent kitchen and seemed to pause in front of the refrigerator door. He closed the refrigerator and opened the freezer for ice, dropped the cubes into a short glass and filled it halfway with bourbon.

When he returned he took a large swallow and placed the glass on the coffee table. "I've never told anyone but Eric about the rings."

"What are the rings?"

Lanny spoke slowly, the frown wrinkles around his eyes not matching the smile on his lips. "It started after my first confirmed kill. We worked house to house clearing out tiny opposition cells, so our kills were all up close," he said, looking at the wall opposite the couch. "You're not going to want to hear this."

"Yes, I do. You never told me about that part of the war. I want to know about it. It's fine." Lizzy slid over on the couch and placed a hand on his chest. She could feel the long scar beneath his tee shirt than ran the length of his rib cage, from surgery to remove shrapnel.

"The best rule is, you don't talk about that stuff. It's not good to talk about it with someone who wasn't there."

Her finger traced the scar upward. Then she put her hand at the back of his thick neck and massaged it a moment as she spoke, "I need you to talk about it."

Lanny concentrated on the wall or ceiling and only took quick glances at Lizzy as he explained how his unit worked in teams of three going house to house. He was teamed with two experienced soldiers who were on a second tour. When they kicked in a front door of a house one day, a gun fight followed with men inside the house. Lanny killed one of the two; one of his partners killed the other.

"My buddy walked over to the dead guy that he had shot and cut a square of cloth from the man's shirt." Lanny took a swallow of bourbon and put the glass back on the coffee table. "I asked what he was doing. He said be cool, it wasn't a trophy, just a way to remember what it was like over there."

"I see," Lizzy said. She sat sideways on the couch with her legs folded under her, her back straight, just inches from Lanny. He hands were now quiet in her lap.

"The other guy with us said he took a bullet from the gun of anyone he killed. And they both looked at me to see what I thought," Lanny said, reaching for his glass of whiskey. He swirled the ice around in the glass.

"What did you say?"

"You have to understand, Lizzy. It's scary over there. Someone has to have your back, and they had mine. I had to show I was one of them."

"Oh, I get it. You took a dead man's ring?" she said, reaching over and gripping his right hand for emphasis. She held his hand up and said, "You don't even wear a ring." As if that somehow made the situation more puzzling.

He pulled his hand away from Lizzy. "That's where it started. At that moment, I was in or I was out." He tilted his glass back and finished the last few drops of bourbon in one gulp.

"I walked back to the guy stretched out on the floor and looked at him for something I could take. He had a ring, so I slid it off his finger and put it on my spare bootlace like a necklace. They cheered."

"So did you do it any more?" Lizzy looked at Lanny, her mouth open.

"Six times."

"Let me get this right. You killed seven men? And took their rings?"

Lanny nodded, saying nothing more. Looking down into his empty glass.

Lizzy caught herself biting her thumbnail and stopped, putting her hands back in her lap. "Well, that's kind of creepy, but I guess I don't see why it's that bad under the circumstances. I guess you got rid of the rings, right? When you came back, I mean."

Lanny looked at Lizzy and shook his head side to side, his eyes glistening and red.

"You don't mean you still have the rings from a bunch of dead guys do you?" She asked, but it was more accusation than question.

****

Lizzy awoke when Lanny threw back the covers. She rolled over and checked the clock. Two in the morning. "Bad dreams again?" she asked, as Lanny sat across from her with his feet on the floor. The thin curtains, backlit from the streetlight, cast a light blue tint on the room, and where the cloth did not meet in the middle a thin wall of pale light cut across the foot of the bed. The light was enough to make out Lanny standing up and trying to put on his jeans.

"Just can't sleep," he said, the frustration obvious in his voice.

She had noticed that Lanny would occasionally get up in the night, but she'd gone through such periods in her life and said nothing. Now Lanny's sleepless nights seemed to come more often. Twice this week already she had awakened, and Lanny was nowhere in the house. He had come home an hour or two later, saying he had to walk it off to get back to sleep. For a week Lizzy had avoided bringing up the subject of the rings, wondering if the increased sleeplessness was mere coincidence, or had the dreams gotten worse since she brought up the rings? She hated arguing and knew that her distaste for the rings had brought them close to a fight when she had asked to see them. Lanny refused, saying they were "packed away somewhere" with his military clothes and equipment.

"How about I rub your back? Would that help?" she offered. She reached over and ran her hand across his shoulders, but he stood up out of her reach.

"I just need a walk."

Lizzy lay there awake for an hour, before pulling the cover tight around her neck and finally sliding back into dreams before Lanny returned.

****

Lizzy knelt beside the flower bed Lanny had dug in her front yard. She smoothed black dirt around the last lantana planted along the stones that edged the plot, patting the dirt with the back of a trowel. She planted the trowel into the soft earth of the flower bed and removed her baseball cap. Her short, damp hair stuck to her head where the hat band pressed against her scalp.

"Is there some reason we picked July to do this kind of work?" Lanny shouted from the other side of the yard, where he was turning over earth for a second bed she wanted.

Lizzy laughed.

"I'm going to get some ice water. I'll bring you a glass." She pulled her hat on as she walked to the kitchen door.

"That would be great," he said, leaning the long-handled

shovel against a tree and wiping sweat from his face with a red handkerchief. His tee shirt was drenched through and through.

Lizzy stomped her feet on the mat at the carport door and glanced at Lanny. This felt right, down to the dirt under her fingernails. Inside, she added ice to a large plastic pitcher and filled it with water from a bottle of spring water. She grabbed a lemon from the bowl on the white tile counter, pressed it with her palms against the counter top. She sliced it into four wedges, then squeezed the juice into the pitcher and tossed the wedges in with the ice water. She picked up two plastic glasses and the pitcher, thinking of how happy she had been for the past couple of months. Conversations just happened, without her trying to think of something to talk about.

Lizzy carried the water to the wooden picnic table and poured them each a glass as Lanny sat across from her.

"Cheers," Lanny said, toasting her with his water.

"It looks great, Lanny. Thanks for doing the hard part."

"It's fun. I haven't done gardening for years. I used to help my mother a little," he said. He raised one foot up to the bench seat and retied a bootlace on his army boots.

****

Lizzy saw that she was the first one home from work as she turned into the empty driveway. Her disappointment made her realize how much she enjoyed his strong arms holding her when he met her at the front door. She'd been held by a few men, but none had made her feel this way.

When she tried to push open the front door, it stuck halfway open. A stack of mail dropped through the slot that day had formed a paper wedge. She squeezed through the narrow opening, picked up the mail and sorted the stack, placing the most important pieces on bottom. She read through the bills and four-color fliers, and tossed most of them into the trash as she stood next to the kitchen counter. The last piece was a hand-addressed letter. The return address belonged to John's mother.

Lizzy sat at the kitchen table and stared at the envelope without opening it. She realized she had succeeded in not thinking as much of John for the past few months since the anniversary of his death.

She ripped the end off the letter and found a single sheet, neatly folded:

Dear Elizabeth,

I hope this letter finds you well and you have found peace since John's death. I continue to miss him so dearly. He was such a good son and my memories are all good. I know you and John loved each other and you will always hold a special place in my heart. I'm writing to invite you for lunch sometime, when it is convenient for you. Would the end of next week work out for you? I will call early in the week to find a good date.

May God bless you,

Margaret Vance

P.S. John's silver ring with the grape leaf etchings was originally my father's. I would so love to have it, if it's not too much to ask.

Lizzy's arms felt too heavy to hold the letter. Her hands trembled as she reread the words, trying to remember last seeing the ring. John always wore it. She noticed the ring was not on John's hand at the funeral and assumed Margaret had kept it. She'd decided not to say anything at the time, since she and John were not married. She knew the ring was nowhere in her house or in John's personal things, which she had sorted and returned to Margaret in half a dozen new cardboard boxes a year earlier.

Lizzy heard Lanny's truck door shut. She looked at the front door and, without thinking, stuffed the letter into her pocket.

Lanny came through the door and walked straight to Lizzy, bending over to give her a quick kiss. Lizzy turned her face to the side and offered her cheek.

"You all right?" he said. He wrinkled his forehead, focusing on Lizzy's face.

Lizzy knew she couldn't hide being upset. She tried to smile. "I was just thinking of one of the girls from work. I told you about her. Anne. Her cancer is back."

Lizzy felt a sharp pain at her temples. *Why am I lying about this?*

Lanny nodded. He stared down at her for several seconds, then he reached out and placed a hand on her shoulder. "Sometimes things aren't as bad as we think."

****

Lizzy stood near the window in the living room and peered through the tiny opening to watch Lanny drive off to work. The early morning sunlight angled shafts of yellow down through the trees. She dialed Eric's telephone, then hung up after one ring.

She sat on the couch, placing the phone on the coffee table. She had to think. Her thoughts scared her. She was being silly, she told herself. John could have taken off the ring so he didn't lose it camping and somehow it got misplaced. Maybe the rescue or ambulance guys stole it. Maybe it was in his camping gear, and she had just missed it. Lots of things could have happened.

She picked up the phone and hit redial. Eric answered

immediately. "Hello."

"I need to talk to you," Lizzy said.

"You don't sound so good."

"Why did you tell me to ask about the rings?" Lizzy asked, as she walked back to the front window to watch the street.

"I didn't want you to get hurt. He may be my cousin, but he came back from the Marines different. What happened?"

Lizzy hesitated. "Nothing happened."

"Right. You called me at seven-thirty in the morning to ask about Lanny's collection of dead-guy trophies because everything is fine."

"Nothing happened. Honestly," Lizzy said, working hard not to lie to Eric.

Eric was quiet. Finally he spoke, his voice kinder. "Just tell me."

Lizzy switched the phone to her other ear as she walked to the kitchen to pour coffee. She sighed. "I need you to tell me I shouldn't worry about something that's probably nothing and I'm just being paranoid."

Eric laughed. "You can't even make a coherent sentence. Clearly something has you upset."

"It's John. Or his mom I should say. She wrote to ask me for John's ring back."

"His ring?"

"I don't have it," Lizzy said. She picked up her coffee cup, but did not take a sip. "I thought she had it. I noticed he wasn't wearing the ring at the funeral and assumed she kept it."

"And you think Lanny took it?"

"No, I don't think he did," Lizzy said as she sat down at the kitchen table. She paused for a second. "But, I guess I had to wonder. I mean, he found the body. He had the chance. But why would he take John's ring?"

"I don't think I should answer that, Counselor," Eric said.

She hated it when Eric called her that. His joke didn't make her feel any better. "Look, I need to get to work. We'll talk later." She hung up.

Lizzy removed the key to Lanny's apartment from her jewelry box and held it in her palm. Was it worth the risk of driving Lanny away if he'd done nothing? She slid the key into the inside zipper pocket of her purse and decided she could think about the consequences later. She drove to her office.

At eleven-thirty Lizzy dialed Lanny's cell phone. He answered immediately. "Hey Love," Lanny said, recognizing her number.

"Hey, just wanted to know if you had anything in mind for dinner. If you don't, then I'll pick up some things on the way home."

"Anything is fine with me."

"You in the field today?" Lizzy asked.

"Nah, just working in the office."

"Okay, see you after work." Lizzy knew what she needed to know. Even if Lanny was not out cruising timber, he was far from his apartment. The Land Company office was fifteen minutes outside the Huntsville city limits and all the way across the city from there. She pushed herself back from her computer, reached for her purse and told the receptionist she might be a little late getting back from lunch.

Inside Lanny's apartment, Lizzy searched for the rings on a bootlace. She looked inside drawers, careful as to how things were placed and leaving them just as she found them. The apartment held little. Lanny had not bothered to unpack many of his belongings that had been placed in storage when he left for his military service, and he had told her that some of the things he brought back from the army were also put in storage. In fifteen minutes she had looked through the bedroom, searching the bedside table and the one chest of drawers. Nothing.

The living room held only a couch, a small coffee table and a bean bag chair.

She moved to the kitchen and rummaged through every drawer, though half held nothing. One was filled with new flat-ware simply dumped inside, with no dividers. Another held the normal miscellaneous kitchen items: masking tape, box of matches, screw driver, pliers, candles, and a cork screw.

She looked around the living room again and saw the coffee table had a small drawer. Inside she found a key with a small round paper label that said 406. On the other side it read, Gate code: 1597# 9406*. Lanny had once pointed out to her the rental storage he used. It was only two blocks away. She looked at her watch. She had time.

A blast of hot air hit Lizzy as she pushed up the rental stor-age room door. Inside were a few straight-back chairs, a floor lamp, fishing rods standing in a corner, an exercise bike, and a dozen or so boxes. She thought Lanny could have used the chairs and lamp in his sparsely furnished apartment. The boxes were unmarked, but three sitting to one side had military shipping labels. She felt her shirt stick to her back as she bent to read the labels.

Fortunately, each of the boxes had already been neatly cut open. The first box contained nothing but military fatigues. Inside the second she found a shoe box among various papers and civilian clothing. She felt her heart rate increase as the removed the box and heard a small tinkling sound. Inside was a black bootlace holding seven rings of various styles. Most were simple gold or silver bands. She closed her eyes and exhaled a long breath when John's ring was not among the collection. *Lizzy,* she thought to herself, *you're paranoid. Get over it.* A drop of sweat ran down her cheek.

****

"You don't seem like yourself," Lanny said. He and Lizzy sat rocking on the front porch swing. They were sipping red wine and watching the sun fade behind the tall oaks that lined the sidewalk down to the corner. "You've been distracted all week. What's wrong?"

Lizzy thought about her answer. She had not said anything about the letter from John's mom, and the longer she said nothing the worse it would be if Lanny found out. "It's nothing really. John's mother wrote me and asked about a ring he used to wear."

Lanny put his feet down and stopped the swing, turning to Lizzy. He looked hard into her eyes, saying nothing. Finally he said, "I see."

"It's nothing. I'm sure the ring is just misplaced."

"I get it," Lanny said, his voice cold and flat. "How long ago did you get the letter?"

Lizzy's heart surged into her throat. She swallowed hard and tried to sound cheerful and unconcerned. She shrugged as she answered, "A couple of days. I just forgot to mention it."

Lanny nodded. Then he rose and walked inside, saying nothing.

When Lizzy entered the house a few minutes later, she saw

he had a large zippered travel bag open on the bed. She stood at the door as he crammed his underwear and tee shirts into the bag. The scene was oddly familiar, though before it had been the man standing in the door watching as she packed clothes in anger.

"You're leaving."

"You're very observant," Lanny said, not bothering to look at Lizzy as he opened the closet and grabbed several shirts hanging there and a pair of boots from the floor.

"Lanny, why are you so upset? I don't understand." Lizzy walked to the bed and sat next to the overflowing bag of clothes.

"I went by my apartment this afternoon to pick up some more clothes. I was thinking I should let the place go and make the move permanent, like you said you wanted."

He stopped and turned toward Lizzy, holding a pair of folded blue jeans in his hand. "The little old lady two doors down commented on my pretty girlfriend who had stopped by a few days ago."

Lizzy's shoulders slumped. She lowered her head.

Lanny stuffed the jeans into the bag and forced the zipper closed. He looked up at her and said, "I was waiting, giving you a chance to mention what you had been doing. It doesn't take a genius to figure it out now."

Lizzy still sat on the bed, wondering if she had caused all the problems of the past few years herself, when she heard Lanny lock the door behind him.

****

Eric found a parking space near the side door of the Garden Delight. "We're in luck," he told Lizzy, who was already unbuckling her seat belt before he turned off the truck engine. During the short drive from Lizzy's house, where Eric had picked her up for dinner, they had talked only about work and the relentless heat of the past few weeks.

Eric and Lizzy sat across from each other in a booth about midway along the front window inside the Garden Delight. Although the sun would soon be down, the heat rising from the asphalt parking lot and concrete sidewalk still made it too uncomfortable to sit outside.

Eric reached over and put his hand on Lizzy's hand, forcing her attention to him. "How are you? You okay?"

"Yeah, I'm fine," Lizzy said.

Eric saw a smile on her face, but not in her eyes. "Have you heard anything from Lanny?"

Lizzy pulled her hand away and opened her menu. "He came by when I was at work yesterday and took the last couple of things that were his. He left his key to my house, but we haven't spoken since he left two weeks ago."

"I'm sorry. I didn't want you to get hurt, but I tried to tell you he was kind of explosive like that."

Lizzy recognized the server who appeared at the table.

"Hi, I'm Albert. Can I get you guys some raspberry tea while you decide? It's fresh brewed."

"Can you give us a second, Albert?" Lizzy closed her menu.

Lizzy looked at Eric. She wondered why he assumed this was her favorite place, just because she'd invited him here once. "Eric, I can't stomach another boring salad with fruity tea. Can we go get a burger somewhere?"

Eric laughed and put down his menu. "I've got just the place."

"You don't mind?"

"Do I look like someone who prefers sliced pears, nuts and baby spinach leaves over a burger?"

They both laughed.

It was a ten-minute drive to Mabel's, down roads that grew narrower and seemed to be forgotten by the city's pothole repair crew. After downing cheeseburgers and fries layered in gravy, Lizzy and Eric each ordered a second beer. The tiny window air conditioner made more noise than cool air.

A young black man wearing a Michigan basketball jersey cleared their table, wadding the paper placemats and napkins and dumping everything into a plastic tub. When clean, the pine table revealed dozens of names and initials carved into its surface.

Lizzy held her bottle by the neck and leaned forward with her elbows on the wooden table. "Eric, I know there's not much to tell them, but should I say something to the police about the ring?"

Eric peeled the beer label with his thumbnail, considering the question. "I'm not sure. What would you say?"

"Well, just that John's mother and I don't know where the ring he always wore might be."

Eric sipped his beer and placed the bottle on the table. "What about Lanny? Do you tell them about his rings?"

"I'm not sure. I think I have to. I'm certainly not accusing anyone of anything, but it seems like I have to say something."

Eric nodded but did not speak.

They finished their beers. Eric left cash on top of the bill, including a five dollar tip, though they'd had to yell into the kitchen for Mabel to bring them their second beers.

As Eric walked beside Lizzy he slid his left hand into the

pocket of his jeans. He opened Lizzy's door with the other hand and held it for her. She looked at him for a second as she paused on the step-up, as if to speak, but she said nothing. He smiled, their faces inches apart. Lizzy slid onto the seat. Eric closed the door gently, pushing until he heard the latch click. As he walked around the back of the truck, he felt the silver ring deep in his pocket. With Lanny out of his way, why risk keeping it? He'd toss it to the bottom of the Paint Rock River on his way home. He rolled the band between his fingers, tracing the intricate engravings with a fingertip.

Acknowledgements

T

o the editors and publishers where some of these stories first appeared, you have the author's heartfelt thanks, especially to Sonny Brewer for including "The Turkey Hunt" in the anthology *Stories from the Blue Moon Café IV*, which represented my first fiction accepted for publication. "Maybe this'll get you started," you said. My appreciation to these magazines: *storySouth* ("And it Burned," now titled "The Downtown Club"); *Southern Gothic* ("Charisma"); and *Thicket* ("To Be Loved in Skyline"). For reading endless early versions of many of these stories and for your criticism both gentle and stern, I must thank Cindy White and Anita Miller Garner. Even when the stories had buck teeth, smudged faces and obnoxious personalities, you knew they were my children and you praised them for what they could become while pointing out how they might improve their behavior. For that kindness and incalculable improvements in the stories, I'm indebted. And special thanks to Anita for giving me Rocky for the Willie Greene story. I had no idea he'd end up a killer. For creating spectacular cover designs from which to choose, kudos to the South's greatest designer, Bill Porch. For staying up late at deer camp to allow me to test story ideas, thanks to Andy and Deb. For letting me read story drafts out loud during the past four years of Dauphin Island vacations together, thanks to Charles and Lynda. Let's do it again this summer—I have a manuscript about Elvis I want to ask about... To J.B and Joe, thanks for letting me tell about your ill-fated turkey hunt. (Just for the record, they're not brothers, never dated the same woman and would never shoot a caged bird.) To Jeanie Thompson, for guidance and for many introductions to people who serve up encouragement to live the writing life. My admiration and thanks to my editor Henry Oehmig for his perfect mix of correction and suggestion. To my publisher David Magee, thanks, not just for choosing the book, but for your enthusiasm and determination to make the process fun. To my wife Virginia, in addition to taking time from your painting (www.virginiashirley.com) to read my drafts and ask if I "really meant to say this?", how can I repay you for the lost vacation hours, uncut grass, late nights with the lights on and early mornings when the artist in you told the wife in you to give me space to work?

Everyone mentioned herein made a positive difference for this work in some way. Any mistakes that remain are solely mine.